To

Best regards,

Jeanine Malarsky

UNWORTHY

by Jeanine Collins Malarsky

Cambridge Books
an imprint of
WriteWords, Inc.
CAMBRIDGE, MD 21613

Cambridge Books is a subsidiary of:

Write Words, Inc.
2934 Old Route 50
Cambridge, MD 21613

ISBN 1-59431-853-0 or 978-1-59431-853-5

Fax: 410-221-7510

Bowker Standard Address Number: 254-0304

Dedication

I dedicate this book to my dear classmate, Barbara Fry Conner, for her encouragement and friendship. She is a shining example of the positive value of religion: she pursues a doctrine of her choice but embraces those who don't.

Acknowledgements

I want to express my gratitude to three professionals for their valuable assistance in my research for this book:

Daniel G. Cronin, Detective
Criminal Investigations Division
North Andover Police Department
North Andover, Massachusetts

Jan Cowan, Case Management Supervisor
Commonwealth of Massachusetts
Department of Mental Health

Cathleen Crowley, Journalist

CHAPTER 1

A Brass Key

Vengeance was the last thing on Rachel Vogel's mind as she tied her apron strings securely behind her back and pulled her new canister vacuum from the utility closet in the kitchen. Tugged by its hose, the sleek, pearl gray machine followed her, its small plastic wheels clicking over the patterned linoleum floor. She smiled to herself as she recalled her mother's old Electrolux gliding along on its chrome runners, the exhaust hole in its butt spewing ancient dust. Her smile faded as she remembered choking on the filthy dust cloud when she had to empty the old fabric bag, reaching her arm up inside to invert the bag and beat it against the foundation of the house. She was so grateful that her husband Butch had allowed her to buy this updated model with its retractable cord, vibrating carpet head, and disposable dust bags.

She frowned momentarily as she navigated the dining room, its scarred wood floor in desperate need of a carpet. In the lord's good time, she comforted herself. She plugged the vacuum cleaner cord into an outlet in the living room wall next to the low bookcase. Her eyes passed over the three shelves of books, used, but treasured. As she stepped on the round gray button, the motor roared to life and her thoughts strayed to Butch over at the church, working with a crew of faithful members who had volunteered to paint the basement rooms over the weekend. She could see why he was well liked: he never refused to help.

She directed the thrumming cleaner head with its pulsing rubber rollers over the fern and floral pattern of the carpet, taking care not to scuff the legs of the furniture, though most of it was used, some from her parents and some from other church members willing to help young families get established.

Rachel unconsciously averted her eyes from the three paintings on the walls, all wedding gifts from her father: a wind-torn young woman rowing a boat into a storm, three frightened horses rearing back from lightning bolts aimed toward their eyes, and a yellow-tinted blackish painting of a dying Indian. Her father had insisted she hang them where they could be seen and admired. But she'd learned to not see them; she hated them.

She did her household chores with great care this sunny morning of July 11th, 1976. The fatigue from sleep deprivation that had been gnawing away at her core for the past six months gave way to happy memories of the day trip Butch and she had taken the day before.

As she vacuumed and reminisced about the previous day, she began to hum "This Little Light of Mine," a tune she treasured from her childhood. Like a loving couple they had strolled through Faneuil Hall snacking on yogurt and fresh strawberries. Then they had joined thousands of residents and tourists near the New England Aquarium to watch the *USS Constitution* lead the Tall Ships parade through Boston Harbor to celebrate the bicentennial of the United States of America.

She cherished her memories of yesterday, clutching them close inside her as she bent to vacuum under the couch. Butch had been so lighthearted and considerate, escorting her gallantly across streets, wiping bits of yogurt off her face and calling her his little owl, like he'd done during the short weeks of their courtship.

"Won't let Satan blow it out," Rachel sang softly as she shoved the vacuum cleaner away with her foot and vacuumed around the coffee table. "What's that?" he asked herself out loud as a rattling sound rose from the vibrating rollers. Instinctively her foot found the gray off button and the motor wound down into silence. She stooped over, lifted the cleaning head and shook it. A tiny brass object fell to the carpet, catching a ray of mid morning sun pouring through the open window.

She plucked the small key from the green nylon fibers of the carpet where it had been hiding and stood up, turning it over and over in her hand and studying it closely. Unlike any other surface in her home, it was blemished by spots of rust. This must be the key to Butch's family Bible she thought. *I wonder if he knows he's lost it.*

She stepped over the vacuum hose and took a seat on the faded crushed velvet couch, locking her gaze on the thick antique Bible in the center of the coffee table. With its worn tooled leather covers it looked more like a leprosy victim than a treasured heirloom.

"It's the only thing I have left of my mother," Butch had told her when he'd brought it home three years before. "When I leaf through the pages and see her entries for her marriage and my birth, the ink black and fresh against the older entries in fading brown, it brings tears to my eyes."

He'd placed the Bible gently on the coffee table and said, "I'd like to keep it here where I can see it every day. It's all I have left to remember her by."

"May I look through it with you?" Rachel had asked, noting the wide strap with its brass clasp was securely locked.

"You know how my mother died," Butch had said, his eyes tearing up as he'd looked into her eyes for understanding. "I'm not ready to share this with anyone yet. Perhaps another time."

Rachel grasped the tiny key between her thumb and forefinger, closed one eye and peered into the minute hollow barrel. She stared at the Bible and back at the innocuous key. *What harm could come from just a peek? Oh, no, I mustn't. I'll just lay the key here and tell Butch about it.* She placed the key carefully on top of the Bible and drew her hand back. She stared at the key. *Just a little peek.* As though speed would negate her sin, she leaned forward swiftly, grabbed the key and inserted it into the brass lock. With a quick turn of her wrist the metal clasp fell away.

Through the dull roar of trepidation that beat against her eardrums, she could still hear the soft music from a religious program on the radio in the kitchen. She didn't listen closely to the Sunday morning sermons that radiated their exhortations to obey God and love thy neighbor, but she liked to tune in so she could enjoy the choral music and the powerful, deep-throated organs that echoed through the great churches from which the sermons were broadcast.

She gently lifted the thick cover, feeling as though she were invading the most intimate parts of her husband. Guilt threatened to attenuate her courage, reminding her that sneaking behind her husband's back was against his explicit instructions. It was also against God's wishes. It was a sin to violate Butch's privacy. Perhaps the Bible's contents will bring us closer, she argued with herself. I know so little about him. The emotional chasm between them since the day they'd been married had always haunted her thoughts. Now it teased her to continue.

The marbled paper that lined the inside of the padded cover and formed the first page was yellowed, causing the maroon swirls to look like smears of very old, dried blood. She leafed through the first few pages, brittle with age and browned on the edges, like they'd been singed with a match.

Funny, she thought, furrowing her forehead into thin ripples and squinting her eyes at the faded ink as she scanned the first page of family events. No Vogels listed. Silly me, she chided herself. Look at the dates. Of course, I wouldn't even know his grandmother's maiden name. Rachel leafed through two more pages of marriages, deaths, births…1910? That's the last entry? Where is Butch's family, his mother's birth, his own birth?

Rachel shifted her knees aside, pulled the heavy book closer to her and began flipping through Genesis, pages at a time. She saw the begats, as her father called them, and smiled when she skimmed across Methuselah's genealogy and spotted Enoch's name. Her brother had been named Enoch because of the biblical Enoch's righteousness. Methuselah's father Enoch had not seen death. He'd walked with God, which her father had explained meant: He'd been so perfect that God had taken him to heaven without allowing Enoch to experience death. *I wonder if my brother will see death,* she pondered. *He wasn't far from a saint himself.*

She tried to ignore the throbbing in her head as she flipped into Exodus, choosing an obvious break in the splayed pages. The old stitched spine creaked as the book flattened to reveal its contents before her on the low table. A colored 8" x 10" photograph of a little girl lay exposed in the sunlight, the child's alluring smile gazing up at Rachel. Rachel did not smile in return. She instinctively reached out to snatch the picture to destroy it, but withdrew her hand as though a poison adder had sprung from the pages and sunk its fangs into her blue-veined wrist.

A muffled cry rose from Rachel's constricted throat as she tried to reach forward again. More than anything in the world, Rachel wanted to pull her eyes away from the picture and run back in time, to breakfast this morning, to yesterday on the wharf, anywhere but here with her eyes riveted on the innocent child's rosy cheeks above the gauzy lilac camisole, the bare abdomen, the slim, undeveloped hips, and her tiny fingers spreading open the lips of her dewy vulva.

The dull roar in Rachel's ears became a crashing wall of waves bludgeoning her brain, blocking her hearing and blinding her sight. Grasping her heaving stomach, Rachel raced through the dining room, smashed the bathroom door back against the wall and threw the toilet seat upright. With trembling hands she grasped the sides of the cool porcelain bowl, dropped to her knees, and thrust her face downward. She vomited so forcefully that the diluted mixture below splashed upwards and bathed her burning cheeks and perspiring forehead.

With her elbows akimbo, Rachel bowed lower and retched, spewing her breakfast in great gobs of pancake lumps that bobbed fitfully in the blueberry stained water.

As her body disgorged her breakfast, deeper inside, her latent memories—acquiescent from years of smothering and denial—began to disgorge their secrets; horrible secrets, ugly secrets, excruciatingly painful secrets.

She wiped her mouth with fat wads of toilet paper. She flushed the toilet and sat back on her heels to slow the tremors that shook her body. With another wad of toilet paper she swiped at the bits of blue slime clinging to the sides of her shoulder length hair. She cried out as disgust and nausea rolled through her body again. She bent forward and vomited until dry heaves racked her ribs and she could expel no more.

Exhaustion held her prisoner on the bathroom floor, crumpled in a heap beside the toilet. She wept until her tear ducts ran dry, then pushed herself upwards and slithered closer to a wall where she could lean and gasp for breath. She grabbed a towel hanging above her head and rolled over on her hands and knees, using the wet toilet rim to help herself stand up.

When she had completed washing herself and cleaning up the floor around the toilet, she returned to the living room, gripping chairs and touching walls to support her efforts to stay upright. Like a rat drawn to the trap by the smell of fresh cheese, Rachel sat down on the couch, leaned over the shabby Bible and methodically paged through the huge volume, sobbing quietly as she studied each pornographic picture.

Though the girls were a cross-section of races, mostly Caucasian, they were all very young, somewhere in the range of three years to perhaps six. Waves of pain and tortured memories washed through her head as she turned to each succeeding picture. Near the last third of the Bible, her already stunned and shocked mind encountered more than she could have imagined, a Polaroid picture of Charlotte, the little girl upstairs. A slight paralysis held her frozen in time and space as she studied the pose of the angelic, blond-haired child, her intense blue eyes gazing in trust, giving the camera its fair share of her enigmatic smile.

Charlotte's mother and father had rented the upstairs apartment for the past five years. Charlotte's father went away in the Navy for months at a time. When he was between jobs, Butch had always been kind and accommodating to Charlotte's mother, volunteering to baby-sit and making it possible for her to run errands or have an occasional evening out. Charlotte's mother had called Butch, "Sweet." Yes, Rachel thought as she stared at the little girl's picture, everyone loved Butch.

Rachel closed the Bible and carefully locked it. She slipped the key into the deep pocket of her apron and looked around the room, now unfamiliar to her, expanding and contracting as she tried to focus.

Three ceramic birds, perched on the top of her bookcase, rose and fell in her vision like gulls tossed about on stormy waves. Rachel tried to steady her focus on the tin flue cover on the far wall that Butch had painted over when he'd painted the living room two years before. The fluted cover blended in with the tan wall, barely noticeable, yet still reminiscent of the brass flue covers in her parents' home when she'd been little. She winced and shook her head. Being little had hurt. Her brain felt soggy, like thick oozey mud. She could barely think.

The overwhelming urge welling up inside her was to not exist, an old feeling to which she had never found a solution. "The Lord never gives us more than we can bear," she reminded herself in a soft murmur. As though navigating a foreign space, Rachel rose from the couch, grasped the wands and hose and began pulling the vacuum back toward the kitchen. Half way through the dining room, she let her shoulders slump, dropped the wands and hose and stumbled into the bedroom she shared with Butch. Tears welled up again as she looked at the neatly made bed where she had tried to be a good wife. She had failed miserably.

She pulled the bedspread back and folded it carefully, laying it on the faded rose boudoir chair as was her habit each evening. She fell on the bed weeping. How much of her life had she longed for surcease of pain, for the peace that passed all understanding as promised in the Bible? She longed for solace, for comfort. Never, not since she'd been very young, had anyone been there to help her bear her cross. She lay on her side and stared at the small chair, thinking back to the auction where she had purchased it for a dollar. Her mother, Willa, had encouraged her to buy it.

Yes, Willa, her mother, had gone to the auction with her.

She closed her eyes and pictured her mother. Willa Keller was a homemaker, mother of three, minister's wife, church organist, and piano teacher. For Rachel, Willa was a shell; never really there, not when Rachel had needed her. Rachel buried her tear-stained face in the pale green pillowcase and prayed she would never wake up. Though her mother had never shared her inner feelings with her children, Rachel sensed that her mother had also felt this way most of her life, spending endless hours at the church practicing the organ or hiding away from her family in the darkened bedroom, weeping or pretending to be asleep. "Just a little sinking spell," she'd tell her children when they knocked on her bedroom door after school. "I'll get up later and fix supper. Please peel the potatoes and scrape the carrots."

No, Rachel told herself: Willa was no help.

She couldn't talk with her father, even though he was a minister. Weren't ministers kind and loving people? And I do love him deeply, she hurried to remind herself. But she'd never felt comfortable with her father. Fresh tears flowed onto the pillowcase.

What about her siblings?

All through his childhood her older brother had been committed to the ministry. But after his marriage failed he had become a policeman. On occasion she and Enoch talked but when the discussion turned to family and more personal things, she changed the subject. Enoch had introduced her to Butch and she was ashamed to admit she wasn't happy. No doubt Enoch would blame her like Butch did.

And Jessie, her younger sister? Smart, energetic, but impetuous, and so defiant. "She kicks against the pricks," their father said of Jessie's resistant behavior. "She'll burn in hell the way she's going." Rachel often defended her thoughtless sister though she too had caught the lash of her unkind words and self-centered behavior.

Once Jessie had moved into her own place in Boston, she'd had little time for home and family. If Willa asked, Jessie would join them for Sabbath dinner, proof that she did have a kind heart. Maybe, this one time, I could talk with her. Rachel's head pounded as she propped herself up on an elbow and reached for the bedside phone. Maybe this once.

When Rachel heard Jessie's cheery message on the answering machine, she almost hung up. Instead she stayed on the line long enough to leave a brief message saying her call wasn't important and not to worry. She'd been right; there was no one she could talk to. She must carry her own cross. That's what she'd been taught. That's what she would do.

CHAPTER 2

Exit Into Madness

"What the hell are you doing in bed at this hour?" Butch yelled at Rachel from the bedroom doorway. "Where's my supper?" He came closer to the bed and reached out for the phone. Rachel winced. "You can't even hang up a fucking phone. How long's it been off the hook?"

"I fell asleep." Rachel spoke faintly as she forced her swollen eyelids fully open. She pulled her hand from under the pillow and brushed her wispy brown hair off her face. The air felt stifling. Dust motes danced in the low slanting rays of the late afternoon sun.

"I paint goddamn ceilings all day and come home to a lazy bitch who can't move the vacuum cleaner out of the way. I broke my neck tripping over the fucking hose." He returned to his position in the doorway. As was his custom, Butch didn't look Rachel in the eye. He either looked over her head or to the side as he was doing now. "And the house stinks. What's been going on here?" This last question was addressed to the balls along the top of the cheap brass headboard.

Rachel sat upright and tried to collect her thoughts. Butch's harsh words were familiar, his nasty tone, his condemnatory attack; it helped restore her mind to the present.

"I thought you guys were going to play softball when you finished painting," she said. She slid off the bed and slipped past Butch, going into the bathroom to wash her face and comb her hair.

"We lost," he said through the closed bathroom door. "I'm hungry and it looks like you haven't even started cooking."

"I'll be right out," Rachel said through the door.

"Well you'd better hurry." Butch's snarl penetrated the bathroom walls, loud and clear above the running water in the sink. "You promised me chicken cacciatore and I don't see a damned thing going in the kitchen. You can't cook that in five minutes." He returned to the kitchen, grabbed his catcher's mitt and softball from the table and stormed out to the back room where he stashed them high on a shelf.

Rachel avoided looking at Butch as she quickly reached through the kitchen doorway and took the heavy cast-iron skillet from its hook on the wall near the washing machine. Though cast-iron had its role in her cookery, she had relegated the dull black skillets to a wall in the back room where they wouldn't detract from her collection of shiny stainless steel and copper pans on display in her kitchen.

She placed the skillet on the large front burner and went to the refrigerator to get the package of chicken. When Butch reentered the kitchen, he banged the door into Rachel's back as she poked around on the shelves, looking for the thawed chicken. She closed the refrigerator door and gave Butch a frantic glance then opened the freezer door and spotted the white package with the black grease pencil label. She closed the freezer door and looked at Butch in dismay. "I'm sorry, Butch. I forgot to set the chicken out to thaw this morning."

She backed away from the refrigerator and ran her hands down the front of her wrinkled apron in an attempt to control their trembling. Her thin cotton dress added to her fragile appearance. The fear in her eyes was an invitation to Butch's aggressive nature and drew him closer to her.

"What do you mean, you forgot?" He reached out and pushed her back against the sink.

13

"I said, I forgot." Rachel tried to stand straighter and move away. "I'm very sorry. Maybe we can eat the meatloaf left over from Friday night." She tried to duck around Butch and return to the refrigerator. "I think we have some mashed potatoes left also, and I can make up a nice salad."

"You sniveling, lazy bitch," Butch said as he grabbed her left arm and tried to turn her to face him. "Rotting in bed, whimpering and crying about how you can't sleep anymore and how hard you work." Rachel tried to free herself but as she turned away, Butch twisted her arm behind her back and started to press upwards on her wrist. Tears scalded her reddened and swollen eyes; pain exploded through her shoulder. She tried to wrench herself free just as Butch launched her across the kitchen. She bounced off the table and crashed into the tall baker's rack where she stored her carefully shined and polished cookware. She grabbed an upper shelf.

The baker's rack fell forward, emptying its shelves in a cascade of clanging metal. The pots banged and bounced on the floor as Rachel lost her balance and tumbled among them, landing on her twisted arm. Pain shot through her shoulder like a knife ripping through silk.

"Stop it," she whimpered, letting her head droop as she grasped her injured arm. The sensation of oozing mud she'd felt in her brain earlier in the day returned, thickening and solidifying. The kitchen grew darker. Thunderous waves beat against her ears.

Rachel dragged herself toward the stove, pushing the pots out of her way. She grasped a chair and hoisted herself unsteadily to her feet and leaned back against the stove.

Butch grabbed his newspaper off the counter where he'd thrown it earlier and headed for a chair at the kitchen table. He gave Rachel a little smirk and said, "I'll read the paper while I wait. Heat up the meatloaf." He turned his back to her and dropped into a chair. "Hurry up," he said. "I'm starved."

14

Rachel slumped against the stove and stared at the back of Butch's bent head, noticing each tiny brown hair of his crew cut and the robust muscles of his neck, shoulders and upper arms. Though he'd been out of the army for ten years, he still maintained a military haircut and exercised daily. She turned toward the stove but was stopped short by searing pain in her left arm. She braced herself against the stove with her right hand and stared down into the blackness of the iron skillet she wouldn't be needing to cook the chicken.

She took a deep breath and grasped the heavy skillet with her right hand. She must return it to its hook in the back room. As she began to turn away from the stove, a great charge of energy rushed through her body tensing her muscles into a taut spring. She lifted the cast-iron skillet and let it swing away from her body like the ball on a medieval flail. Light as a ballerina in a dance of death, Rachel gracefully swung the skillet in a low arc and crashed it into the side of Butch's head.

The impact with Butch's skull sent fresh waves of pain through Rachel's body, but she couldn't feel them. As though in a trance, she watched Butch slump sideways and tumble out of his chair, sprawling face down among the scattered pots and pans.

The oozing sludge in her brain pressed more heavily but she knew it was important to return the skillet to its hook. As the uneven embroidered words on her first sampler, now hanging on her kitchen wall, read, "*A Place for Everything and Everything in its Place.*" She looked at the sampler hanging by the utility closet, then down at the pool of blood flowing from her husband's head. The blood spread out into threadlike fingers following the depressions in the geometric pattern of the pale linoleum; like a river fanning out across its delta, she thought. Again, searching for a reference to the familiar, she turned her gaze to the other sampler she'd embroidered a year later. "*Cleanliness is Next to Godliness.*"

Vaguely reassured of her bearings, Rachel stepped around Butch's body and went out to the back room. She restored the skillet to its sturdy hook, untied her apron and carefully hung it on its nail near the iron cookware.

She returned to the kitchen and turned off the radio that had been playing softly since morning. She pulled out a chair and sat down at the table, placed her elbows on the table and dropped her chin into her hands. Staring at the worn boomerang pattern on the dull Formica surface, she let her eyes go out of focus and loosened the tenuous grip on her last thread of sanity.

CHAPTER 3

Aftermath

The fluorescent ceiling fixture cast a bluish white glare on Rachel's dull brown hair hanging limply across her cheeks. It created shadows on her worn face that aged her beyond her thirty-two exhausting years. The light had gone out of Rachel's pale green eyes so many years before that her expressionless countenance did not frighten her younger sister when Jessie first entered the kitchen.

"Hi, Rachel," Jessie said as she dropped her overnight bag by the door. "How come you didn't answer the front door? Doorbell broken?"

When Rachel did not acknowledge Jessie's arrival, Jessie moved around the table as she cast her eyes about the kitchen, in search of a clue to Rachel's silence.

"Oh, my god!" escaped from Jessie's mouth though she made it a rule to avoid swearing in the presence of her family. "Oh, my god!" she said in quiet awe of the scene before her. On the other side of the table were the fallen baker's rack, the scattered pots and pans, and Butch, scarlet blood still flowing from his head wound.

Creeping more to her right, Jessie studied the chaotic mess on the kitchen floor while she chastised herself for being so unobservant. What a fool! This is how I make a living! She stepped over the cookware, and bent down to touch the carotid artery in Butch's neck. He lay on his stomach, his head angled oddly to the side. Stone dead, she thought. Wow! Rachel must have hit him a good one. Jumping upright Jessie exclaimed out loud, "My god! You killed Butch!"

Turning back to the table Jessie threw her arms around Rachel, crying in her ear, "Rachel, oh Rachel. What have you done? What happened here? Did he hurt you? Oh my god, Rachel." Rachel was no more responsive to Jessie than a mannequin in a store window. "I need time to think," Jessie murmured as she pulled herself away from Rachel and went over to stand near the baker's rack. Wait a minute. What if someone else did it? What if they're still in the house? Though her instincts argued for her first assumption, she made a swift circuit of the bedroom, living room and dining room. Returning to the kitchen, she bent down and lifted the heavy rack to an upright position and pushed it back against the wall. She looked around then walked thoughtfully toward the door to the back room. She assured herself the outside door was securely closed then reentered the kitchen and closed the door to the back room. No, she told herself, my first impression is correct. This was between Rachel and Butch. I need to think.

Think. That was what she needed to do. "This is a crime scene," she said out loud struggling to engage some clear mental processing. She scanned the room again and let her eyes rest on Rachel's bowed head. Palpable waves of old guilt enveloped her. She shook her head slightly to dislodge her muddled thoughts. "I have to call the police."

As she reached for the phone on the kitchen wall, her hand was stayed by a voice in her head saying, Not yet. You can't just call the police and tell them outright that your sister has killed her husband. For Christ sakes, what will happen to her? She can't even speak.

Jessie crept closer to Rachel and put her hand on her sister's shoulder. "Rachel," she said. "Rachel. Please talk to me." Again the waves of guilt swept over Jessie, threatening her composure as she bent down and peered into Rachel's vacant eyes. "I did this to you," Jessie said, tears of shame forming in her eyes. "This is all my fault." She patted Rachel's shoulder futilely. "If I hadn't written that terrible story and gotten you in so much trouble, you'd have never married this piece of scum." Jessie straightened up and scanned the kitchen frantically. The room was so quiet. "What in the hell are we going to do?" she cried out in the damning silence. "Oh, my god, this is real!"

Jessie grabbed a chair from against the wall and sat down at the table close to Rachel. She grasped Rachel's right wrist and tried to break it free from the frozen pose, hoping Rachel wouldn't fall forward and hit her head. With some resistance, Rachel's arm came forward but her chin remained resting on her left hand and she continued to stare blankly ahead.

Uncharacteristically, Jessie burst into tears. Holding Rachel's right hand, rubbing the palm and forearm, Jessie pleaded with Rachel.

"Talk to me, Rachel. Please. Talk to me. I need to know what happened. I think I know, but I'm scared."

Inside her confused mind her alter ego emerged, wearing a slight sneer tinged with triumph. Don't you think you'd better calm down and process this situation a little more rationally? You're the *big* reporter, aren't you? Isn't this the kind of story you'd kill for? Uh-oh, wrong phrase. Anyway girl, you'd better get a grip on yourself. You're the first one on the scene and you'd better get your smarts working.

She stared into Rachel's empty eyes, like looking into a translucent vacuum. She's gone, Jessie thought to herself as she let out the breath she'd been holding without realizing it. She's nowhere.

Jessie rubbed her sister's arm absentmindedly while she reined in her chaotic thoughts. There was a story here but it could cost Rachel. What had Rachel ever done to deserve this? If the truth came out, what would happen to Rachel? She would never survive a murder trial. She would die in prison. Something had to be done to protect Rachel; she looked so fragile. Obviously she'd lost her ability to cope. Was she just in shock? Was her sanity gone? She doesn't move. Had she really gone crazy? Oh my god!

As Jessie scanned the tiny grooves in the painted wainscoting and let her eyes follow along the chair rail in search of answers, an idea struck, presenting itself so clearly it startled her. No, I can't do that, she argued back. She shook her head to dislodge the thought that was forming. Her meticulously cut black hair flared away from her head then resettled into its pristine shape. Her over sized gold hoop earrings quieted their frantic dance and rested gently against her neck. She won't survive. I'm sure of that. She scanned the murder scene one more time, taking in the details. Would my story be convincing? Jessie stared into the darkness of the dining room. Why not? I've covered a few criminal stories. Sat through two trials. For Christ sakes, idiots make it through law school. I can run circles around those egotistical, conniving lawyers. And most cops aren't Mensa candidates. Why wouldn't my story work? Besides, they'll *never* convict me.

The excitement of a great solution, and a less distinct but nonetheless tangible sensation of self-immolation, gripped her emotions. She clenched her fist and hit the table with conviction. I'm strong. I'm experienced. They'll have to believe me. I'm careful about details, accurate to a fault. I'm precise and have an excellent memory. By god, this will work.

Constrained by a slight sense of hesitation Jessie reached out and toyed with the salt and pepper shakers lined up against the shiny gold plastic napkin holder in the middle of the table. She reviewed her premise. She rotated the salt shaker slowly, then took it into her palm and gripped it tightly. I can do this, she told herself. I can do this. I have no choice. I owe this to Rachel. I'm the only person who can save her. I'd better hurry.

Jumping up from the table, Jessie grabbed her bloated leather purse from the counter and plopped it on the table, removing her ever-present notebook as she sat down. I'll write everything down as it happened. I'll get all the details in order and memorize them. Then I'll call the police.

Jessie grabbed a crumpled pack of cigarettes from her open purse and dug into a small pocket for her lighter. Oops. She stuffed her smoking kit back into her purse and reached into another pocket for a fresh pack of gum. She never smoked in front of her family, not that Rachel would notice it now.

Jessie chewed her gum slowly and studied the room; writing notes rapidly, using the inscrutable shorthand she'd developed to catch the essence of events in a rush. At intervals she got up and walked behind Rachel to study the position of Butch's body, then returned and continued writing. Again she rose to study a heavy copper frying pan near his sprawling right arm. "Good lord!" she exclaimed out loud. "That's the pan I gave her last Christmas!"

I wonder if she ever used it, Jessie mused as she resumed writing. Use of Rachel's cookware was hard to assess because every one of the pots and pans was polished to a high sheen. The stainless steel reflected light and the copper glowed. Oh well, Jessie said to herself, she apparently got some use out of it. It's obvious it's the murder weapon.

She studied the first draft of her story, frowning at some of the steps. She rewrote it. She felt satisfied with her fourth version, wadded up the earlier attempts and committed the final to memory. She stuffed her notes into her purse, jumped up from the table and grabbed the pan from the floor, laughing at herself as she headed for the sink. I'm thinking like a detective. I'd better act a bit more excited when the police arrive. Grabbing a dishtowel from a small rod, she vigorously rubbed the brass handle of the heavy tin-lined copper pan to remove Rachel's latent fingerprints. Then, setting the pan on the counter, she carefully gripped the handle and gently swung the pan through the air.

"Perfect." She returned the pan to its original position on the floor and stood back. She bent down to look closely at Butch's quiescent face, expressionless for once. "You prick. Whatever happened here, you deserved what you got."

Stepping carefully around the scattered cookware, Jessie went to the phone and dialed the operator. In a breathless voice she said, "Give me the police. This is an emergency."

***

Before Jessie could complete her first rehearsal, the front doorbell rang. Though she had planned to act shocked and excited, she didn't need to draw on her old thespian talents as she recognized the handsome police officer and threw herself into her brother's arms.

"Oh, Enoch!" Jessie cried as her brother gripped her in a bear hug. "It's so awful!"

"What happened?" Officer Keller asked Jessie, pulling her with him through the long entry hall and across the shadowy dining room toward the lighted kitchen. His partner was right behind him, pulling on Enoch's sleeve.

"Slow down, buddy," Officer Jackson said. "We agreed I'd go first." Officer Timothy Jackson hopped in front of Enoch and Jessie and held out his arms to stop them in the archway between the dining room and the kitchen. "You two wait right here."

"I killed Butch," Jessie sobbed into Enoch's uniform. "He was beating Rachel and I walked in and didn't think and I grabbed the closest pan and hit him." She gulped back a sob. "He was going to kill her. He beats her all the time. He's a brutal beast." She brushed away tears of anger and fear.

"He's still warm," Officer Jackson said from his position on his knees next to Butch. "Call an ambulance and get backup." He looked directly at Jessie and said, "You need to calm down. That your sister at the table? Is there anyone else in the house?"

While Officer Jackson spoke, he expertly rolled Butch onto his back and began CPR. Between movements, he directed Enoch. "Put her in a chair and check the other rooms. Then help me."

Enoch completed his radio call as he raced through the other rooms, returning to the kitchen in moments. Jessie had calmed down and was sitting quietly at the table, holding Rachel's hand and leaning close to her, rubbing her shoulder and back.

"Poor Rachel," Jessie said softly. "Poor Rachel."

Moments later when the EMTs arrived, Officer Jackson and Enoch gave way. Freed from attending Butch, Enoch quickly pulled up a chair next to Jessie and asked her again, "What happened? Slowly. When did you arrive?"

"Excuse me, Officer Keller," Officer Jackson said. "You need to step back and see to securing the crime scene. Then check with the tenants upstairs. I'll take your sister's statement. We'll get enough flack for you being here as it is."

The spacious old-fashioned kitchen became smaller and suddenly stuffy as it filled with emergency personnel, a stretcher, additional police officers and two sisters, one talking too much and one not talking at all.

Detective Joseph D'nardo entered from the front hall. He stopped at the entry to the kitchen. "Got enough people in the way?" he asked as he took in the scene. "Officer Keller," he said addressing Enoch, "can you step in here please?

"You and I both know you aren't supposed to be here," he said, leaning close to Enoch. "But I understand. Have you touched anything?"

"No sir. I secured the scene and helped Tim with CPR." He looked earnestly at the recently transferred detective who he'd seen occasionally in the locker room and at briefings. They stood eye to eye, both five feet, ten inches tall, trim and serious. "This is awful. I couldn't stay away."

Stepping through the archway, D'nardo asked Enoch, "Who's who?"

"The woman talking to Jackson is Jessie Keller, my younger sister. She's a Boston journalist. She came to visit. When she arrived she found Butch Vogel, our brother-in-law, in a fight with

Rachel, my other sister. That's Rachel at the table. She looks like she's in shock. We've sent for another ambulance to take her to the hospital. Could I go along and watch out for her?"

"You've got parents in town, don't you?" D'nardo said, still speaking in quiet tones. "Call them and have them meet her at the hospital. I'll send Officer Cramer with her. He can keep an eye on her and report back when she starts talking."

While Enoch called his parents from a phone in the bedroom, Detective D'nardo studied Butch's body, now being lifted onto a stretcher and secured with straps.

"Dead?" he asked the EMTs.

"Not our decision," the shorter EMT reminded him. In a whispered aside, the EMT added, "I wouldn't hold dinner for him."

"All right," D'nardo said. "I'll be along to the hospital shortly. Hey, wait a minute!" D'nardo said as two more EMTs tried to enter the kitchen from the back room. "Let these guys clear out of here first. The lady will keep another minute. Jackson?" D'nardo stepped closer to where Officer Jackson sat at the table interviewing Jessie. "Can I speak to you for a minute? Excuse me, Miss Keller."

Moving back toward the archway, D'nardo said to Jackson, "Finish your report, then I'll talk to her. I'm sending Cramer to the hospital with Mrs. Vogel. Totally unresponsive?"

"Hasn't moved a muscle since I arrived," Jackson confirmed. More softly he added, "It's pretty straight forward what happened here. I won't be much longer."

Enoch ended his phone call and rejoined D'nardo in the dining room archway.

"Reach your parents?" D'nardo asked.

"They're headed for the hospital now."

"Clear out all the officers but two," D'nardo instructed Enoch. "Put one at the front and one at the back. Tell the media I'll make a statement after I check things at the hospital. Then make yourself scarce."

"I'd like to stay with Jessie."

"Stay with Jackson, then. Don't nose around."

D'nardo put his hands in the pockets of his gray slacks, leaned back on his heels and scanned the scene: ghastly ceiling light, pale yellow walls, calendar near the phone, and two old-fashioned embroidered samplers with messages quite different from the wall plaque in his former wife's kitchen that had read, *"No Bitchen in the Kitchen."*

He studied the kitchen more closely, staring in dismay at the scattered pots and pans, baker's rack angled—*obviously been moved*—thin stain of blood where Butch's cheek had pressed into the edge of the pool, smeared rivulets, distorted by movement of Butch's body. Damn, he swore to himself. The only perfect crime scenes are on TV. Look at the mess they've made. He looked at Jackson, rising from his chair and ending his interview with Jessie.

"That the pan?" D'nardo asked, pointing to the copper frying pan behind an empty chair.

"That's what she says." Jackson closed his notebook and thanked Jessie. "Detective D'nardo would like to speak with you."

Jessie glanced at the plainclothes detective. "I just gave my statement to Officer Jackson," she said. "Isn't once enough?"

"I'll be brief," D'nardo said approaching the table and sitting down in the chair vacated by Jackson. He followed Jessie's worried glance at Rachel. The EMTs had concluded their initial examination and were placing Rachel gently on a stretcher. It looked like an awkward procedure, like handling a dead body in advanced rigor mortis. Indeed, there was little to show she was alive.

"She'll need her glasses," Jessie said, for the first time realizing Rachel wasn't wearing her Coke bottle prescription lenses. She jumped up and looked around the kitchen, then started to step among the scattered pots and pans.

"You can't go there, Miss," D'nardo said. "Does she have another pair?"

"I don't think so," Jessie said. "They're expensive."

"If they're in that mess, they're evidence," D'nardo said. "She'll have to make it through the night without them. I'll make a note of it." He jotted a note on his small pad and motioned for Jessie to return to her seat.

"Can't this wait?" Jessie asked, turning toward the EMTs who were wheeling Rachel's stretcher through the back door. "I have to go with her. Where can I call you?"

"Not so fast," D'nardo said, rising to escort Jessie back to her chair. "I'm sure you're concerned about your sister. She'll be okay. Your brother called your parents. They're meeting the ambulance at the hospital. I need to speak with you."

Jessie started to retort but closed her mouth and stood her position quietly watching Rachel disappear as the two bustling EMTs navigated the small back room and headed down the four back steps. The screen door closed behind them. Only then did Jessie take in the surreal effect of the house where she stood. Though the sirens she'd never heard had died down, every window in her view was filled with bursts of flashing lights: blue, white and red. It was like a ground level celebration of the Fourth of July.

Without a word, she dashed through the dining room and into the living room to the large bay window that looked out on the sidewalk. There they were, a mob of Jessies in different shapes and sizes, dressed for the July heat and poised with their pencils, pads, microphones and cameras; the media. Like a basilisk looking into a mirror for the first time, Jessie let out a cry of horror and drew the drapes with furious jerks. "Go away!" she screamed through the writhing fabric. "Get the hell out of here!"

Pausing to catch her breath, she stood up as straight as her five feet four inches allowed, took a deep breath, put her shoulders back, and walked back to the kitchen. She blinked her eyes and looked at D'nardo. He was staring at her, as though appraising a car, or a good horse; his manner was neither rude nor intrusive.

Maybe I'm losing my mind, too, Jessie thought as she resumed her seat and gave him an exasperated look. "Let's get this over with."

"I understand you are taking responsibility for the alleged murder of your brother-in-law," D'nardo began.

"Accidental death," Jessie corrected. "I did not intend to kill him when I hit him, but, yes, I am responsible." She watched the detective scratch unreadable notes on his pad. "When I arrived, he was beating my sister and I stepped into the fight to protect her. Simple: defense of another person."

"Can you tell me what happened from the moment you entered the house?"

When Jessie had completed answering Detective D'nardo's questions, D'nardo thanked her and stood up, signaling for Officer Jackson.

"Take her to the station and book her. I'm going to the hospital; I'll see you back at the station. Officer Keller can tag along but no private conversations for them tonight. It may be cut and dried. If it is, let's keep it that way."

Softening his stern tone, D'nardo said to Enoch, "Better yet, you might want to see if you can get off duty and meet your parents at the hospital."

CHAPTER 4

Thou Shalt Not Kill

A night in a jail cell and a morning at the courthouse had left Jessie looking slightly wilted. She'd said little on the drive to the hospital with Enoch. Unpleasant scenes of seeing her parents with a charge of murder hanging over her head had been tumbling around in her tired brain. "I hope Father doesn't hand me one of his index cards and tell me to copy a Bible verse one hundred times like he did when we were kids," Jessie said as she and Enoch exited the hospital elevator at Rachel's floor. She gave Enoch a rueful smile. "I'm sure he thought all the spankings and the preaching and praying would have prevented this happening in his family."

"He will have his say," Enoch said as they approached the hospital waiting room around the corner from Rachel's room. "I'm sure the last thing you need is a lecture about right and wrong." He paused outside the door for a moment and said too softly to be overheard, "I know how much this hurts you, Jessie, and I believe every word you said. I might have done the same thing myself, well, except for, I've been trained to handle those situations, and you haven't. I'm sure you did the only thing you could."

"Oh, Jessie," Willa cried, rushing toward Jessie and Enoch as they entered the faded blue waiting room. High on one wall, two thin, horizontal windows funneled bright noon sunlight into the room. "It's so awful. How could you have done it? What's

28

happened to Rachel? It's all over the papers. Our whole family's ruined!" Willa gripped her younger daughter fitfully as she wept in painful gasps. "The doctors think Rachel is insane, but I know she's not."

"Hello, Father," Jessie said as she gently broke free of her mother and assisted her back to the royal blue plastic chair next to Floyd. "How's Rachel?"

"Not well," Floyd Keller said. He looked at Jessie with a dull but steady stare as a long ray of sun slanted across his rigid shoulders and graying head, boldly displaying his thinning hair. He shifted his gaze to stare Jessie in the eye and said, "How could you murder a man? You broke God's commandment. You took another man's life." He vigorously smacked the Bible clutched in his left hand and said, "It says right here, 'Thou shalt not kill'."

Jessie turned toward her father, taking in the harsh tone of his voice and his cold demeanor. How many times throughout her life had she seen this same man bowed in sorrow, hugging and comforting, and bestowing compassion on members of their church, regardless of their crimes or shortcomings? Incongruous and unfitting to the moment, a slight smile forced itself onto her tired face as she reminded herself: that's right; we're family. We can't be weak or make mistakes. We set the example for others. There is no mercy for us.

She took a few steps backward; this was not the time or place to defend herself to her father. In an effort to calm her emotions, she turned away and sneaked a stick of Big Red gum, knowing she was being selfish but it was her last. She gazed at the faded paintings of overly stylized, long-plumed birds on the opposite wall. There must be a subterranean printing house, she thought, where no sunlight has ever reached, that specializes in colorless prints for hotel rooms and hospital walls. She relaxed her shoulders and looked around for a seat.

Willa continued to weep quietly into her handkerchief as Enoch took the chair on her left and reached for her hand. He was her firstborn and had always been her favorite, her little substitute man-of-the-family.

Jessie took a chair at right angles to the others and plunked her crinkled leather purse on the floor. "When can I talk to Rachel's doctor?"

"You don't need to do that," Floyd said. Jessie recognized the practiced pacing of his words, a method of retaining authority without rousing resistance. "Rachel is being transferred to a mental health facility for a full psychiatric evaluation. Then we'll have a better idea of what's going on. Enoch says you were arraigned this morning, charged with manslaughter."

"Oh, my poor Jessie!" Willa cried out in anguish, reaching futilely in Jessie's direction. "Oh, my poor Rachel." She withdrew her arm and returned to twisting her handkerchief in her fingers.

Enoch put his arm around his mother and pulled her gently to rest on his shoulder. "We'll work things out, Mother," he said. "Try to be calm. We're still gathering information. Has anyone come in and spoken with you since I left to get Jessie?"

As he finished his question, a mental health counselor stepped into the room to discuss transferring Rachel. "Mrs. Vogel's condition remains unchanged. They're sending transportation from Danvers State Hospital around four this afternoon," she said. "We have a lot of paperwork to complete so she'll be here for a few more hours."

"You can't do that to her!" Jessie cried jumping up from her chair. "What do you mean, her condition? She's in shock. I'm sure Enoch told you what happened. She can't be locked up in a mental institution. She needs her family close, and needs counseling. That's all."

"The doctors will decide what she needs," Floyd said. "They can't keep her here. It's already been decided."

Jessie whirled around to face her father. "By you? You're not her legal guardian. Why can't she be transferred to a clinic in

Boston where I can keep an eye on her?" Jessie turned to the counselor and then back to Floyd.

"Seems your *keeping an eye on her* left her with a dead husband." Floyd's look was grim and condemnatory. "How could you have possibly believed Butch would hurt Rachel enough for you to kill him?"

"Hurt her enough? Enough? Are you totally blind to how Butch treats, I mean, treated Rachel?" The tension in Jessie's voice began to reveal her inner convictions.

"I'm sure they had their differences," her father said. "All married couples do. But I've never seen him be cruel to her." Floyd remained calmly seated as he spoke, his eyes following the counselor as she eased herself out of the room. His voice took on an indulgent tone. "I know he teased her about her eyeglasses, and I'm sure he's a bit impatient. Many men who have been in the military can be demanding. Plus, you have to admit: he's had a rough time holding a job since they got married. Vietnam did horrible things to many men." Floyd stopped talking and looked over Willa's bowed head to Enoch, then down at the Bible he held between his hands.

Jessie took a seat then immediately stood up again and faced her father, both hands clenched into fists at her side. "I agree that Butch played Dr. Jekyll in public, but his real MO was Mr. Hyde." She relaxed some of the hostility in her posture and sat down again. "I'm sure you aren't the only person he's humbugged. It took me a long time to catch on. He is slick; I'll give you that. Was slick."

"That's a terrible way to speak of the dead," Floyd said.

"Did he hit her?" Willa asked in a timid voice. "I mean, really hit her?"

"Perhaps we can discuss this another time," Enoch said. "I'm sure there is much we all need to talk about, but right now it's important to take care of Rachel and Jessie."

31

"How come you're not locked up?" Willa asked, curiosity overcoming her fear. "Don't they lock up people who kill people?" She broke into another spasm of tears, clutching at the edges of her sweater. "I'm cold," she said. "The air conditioning is too cold."

"I'm free on bail until the trial, Mother," Jessie said. "But there won't be a trial."

"What do you mean, no trial?" Floyd asked.

"It's just a matter of time and formalities. The charges will be dropped when all the facts are presented. The police have to investigate everything, but when they're done, they'll conclude I acted to save Rachel and the whole thing will be a bad memory."

"I think we need to get Mother home to rest," Enoch said rising to his feet. Floyd stood up and helped Willa stand and exit the room, lending his arm for support as they preceded Jessie and Enoch down the shiny hall with its freshly polished dark green floor tiles. As they turned a corner toward the elevators, a strange thought entered Jessie's fatigued mind. I don't think I've ever seen Father lend Mother assistance before. I don't think I've ever seen them touch each other. Funny.

"See you downstairs," Enoch said as Floyd and Willa entered the elevator, taking up the last two spaces. "Are you going back to Boston tonight?" he asked Jessie as they waited for the next available car. "You probably would like to sleep in your own bed. Our holding cells leave a lot to be desired."

"I could have slept in a rusted out pickup truck in a junkyard and been more comfortable." Jessie stretched her shoulders upward and rotated them slowly. "I'm still stiff. Why don't I stay here with Rachel for a while? When you get Mother and Dad settled at home, maybe you could come back and drive me to Rachel's house to get my car."

Enoch and Jessie entered the elevator and rode down in silence. As they exited, they could see their parents ahead of them, moving down the long corridor toward the exit to the parking lot.

"I know you're eager to get going on finding a good lawyer, but I thought you might stay overnight at Mom and Dad's tonight. I'm sure it would mean a lot."

Jessie grabbed Enoch's arm and slowed her step. "Are you crazy, Enoch?" Jessie looked up at him in disbelief. "You know I never stay in that house. My god, it was like a morgue before. Imagine what it will be like now! I can't believe you can live there after having seen the world and found out about life outside the *cult*."

"You say that like you're referring to Father Divine and the International Peace Mission. Calling a well-established Christian religion like The Circle of Redemption of the World a cult, is simply showing disrespect and contempt. I would have thought you'd have outgrown it by now."

"C.R.O.W.s," Jessie said. "A cult of C.R.O.W.s."

"You may have left the church for a rich, secular life, but you could show some respect when you're around family."

They resumed walking slowly.

"At least I didn't become a minister and lose my faith," Jessie replied, looking up at Enoch with a twinkle in her eye. "We have more in common than you care to admit. No," she continued as she slowed her pace even more. "I have a great deal to see to. I can't stay here. In fact, let me ask you a question, Enoch. Do you think Jesus Christ, in all his infinite love, is going to go to court with me and get me off a manslaughter charge? What is the quote, Matthew, I think, where Jesus said to seek first the kingdom of heaven; have no thought for the morrow for the morrow shall take thought for the things of itself? Trust me, I take a lot of heed for the morrow, and I need to get back to Boston tonight."

Enoch stopped and put his arm around Jessie, pulling her gently out of the flow of people. "I know you think you're a tough little nugget, but how are you doing? You know this is all going to hit you when you stop long enough to realize what you did. It's not every day that a person takes her brother-in-law out of circulation."

"I'm not sure what I'm feeling right now," she said leaning against the cool, dull green walls. "I think I'm running on adrenaline. All I can think of is Rachel and when and if she will recover. She's more at risk than I am." Jessie looked into her brother's face. "I think she always has been. Perhaps it's just my gut, intuition, whatever you call it. Last night I was thinking that we've always gotten along okay, but we've never had a real sister-to-sister relationship, not like some of my other friends' sisters. We never shared any secrets, told each other things that were too bad to tell anyone else, you know, girl stuff, sex, all the things that girls talk about without knowing the facts." Jessie laughed. "Like we were ever going to learn any facts in that house."

They resumed walking. "Mother and Dad are waiting for us," she said, looking down the long hall to the glass exit doors where their parents stood outlined in the bright sunlight. They appeared as black cutouts, stiff and resilient, able to weather any storm.

"Call me at the nurses' station in a couple of hours," Jessie said at the door. Her stomach rumbled so loudly that Enoch heard.

"You'd better go to the cafeteria and get something to eat," Enoch said. "Jail food isn't all it's cracked up to be, even if it does come from McDonald's."

"Actually, I haven't eaten since last night."

Enoch left with his parents and Jessie turned back to find the cafeteria. I should go sit with Rachel, Jessie thought, but I doubt she'd notice if I were in the room or not. The thought caused a tiny pain in her chest as she passed the tidy optical shop and the cluttered gift shop. Wow, I've never had chest pains before. She slowed her rush toward the cafeteria. She always walked fast, often outstripping people much taller than her. Maybe this is what they call stress, she told herself with a little laugh. I always thought people imagined it.

In line at the food counter, Jessie turned to the white-coated lab technician behind her and said, "I wonder why a hospital offers dessert before the healthy foods." The lab tech mumbled a response but Jessie wasn't listening. She could still see her parents silhouetted against the sunlit glass doors. Could they weather any storm? What had made her think that? Maybe she was wrong to assume. She knew so little about their background. Her grandparents had died while her father had been posted to Buffalo. She couldn't remember seeing them once. And what did she know about her parents' personal lives?

CHAPTER 5

Honor Thy Father and Thy Mother

In a thumbnail curve of the Ohio River as it swung along Kentucky's left rump, lay a quiet college town, host to Recovery University. The college and seminary for the Circle of Redemption of the World served students from Ohio, Illinois, Indiana and Kentucky. Recovery was a jewel set in a serene valley about thirty miles across the river from Evansville, Indiana.

It was Wednesday, December 18, 1940. Classes had ended by noon to allow the students to make their long drives home for Christmas vacation. The custom was for students living near each other to pool rides with those lucky enough to have cars. Though Floyd Keller was in his first semester at the seminary, he had arranged to drive three students from the undergraduate school home since they all lived in the same area and attended the same church. With weather warnings promising dire driving conditions, some students had left the night before, including two of the girls scheduled to ride with Floyd.

Willa Miller was a freshman, pursuing a degree in teaching and music. Floyd was studying to become a minister, focusing his energies on the youth programs within the religion.

"You look like a drowned rat," Floyd said as Willa threw her suitcase in the trunk and jumped into the passenger seat. Already her wool coat had taken on the odor of wet dog.

"They should allow you to drive closer to the dorm," she said. "I'm drenched."

"You'll dry out," Floyd said as he patted the dash and tweaked the choke of his '36 Chevrolet. "She's not new but she's got a Heat Master; we'll be toasty." He made small talk while he drove through the quiet streets of Recovery heading toward the narrow blacktop road connecting to the main highway. They would turn northeast, pass through Louisville and continue toward home in Clairdale, Ohio. With any luck and hopefully a break in the weather, they'd be home by late evening.

They rode together quietly, trying to catch snatches of music through the static on the radio. Willa's secret excitement in riding home with Floyd was diminishing in direct proportion to the strengthening of the storm. Gray skies had turned black. Except for day bright flashes of lightning, the road was invisible through the sheets of rain that swept across the windshield.

Willa let her eyes follow the frantic efforts of the wiper on the driver's side while a deluge washed over her half of the windshield. She had been ecstatic when she'd heard the other two students had left early. All the night before she'd lain awake thinking about the long hours alone in a car with Floyd Keller, the catch of the Clairdale congregation, the guy that all the other girls drooled over and whispered about, the man Willa had sighed over in private.

Floyd and Willa had both attended the Clairdale church school for years. He was four years older and had never noticed her existence; Willa, with the pleasantly plump body, straight black hair and slightly buck teeth. She'd never had a date. It was good just to be there beside such a handsome young man, a man six feet tall with wavy black hair, a man who was devoting his life to God. In her peripheral vision she could see how he held his head, erect and purposeful, like a Roman centurion. She stole a glance at his firm jaw and her heart raced. She rubbed her hand on the mousy-textured brown upholstery and tried to calm her nerves as she stared straight ahead in a futile effort to help Floyd see the road more clearly.

***

When the state police found the cold car in a deep ravine, they shined their bright oversized flashlights into the foggy windows and banged on the glass. Floyd came sharply awake and pushed Willa to the other side so he could roll the window down, forgetting he couldn't. They had been trapped in the car and had fallen asleep while praying to be rescued.

The trooper motioned for Floyd to move away from the door, then broke the window with the butt of his flashlight. With help from the officers, the two young people climbed out of the ravine and crawled into the waiting patrol car, eager for the precious heat. They sat in the back seat, trembling with chills that penetrated their bones.

"Lucky this is rain and not snow," the trooper in the front seat said. "You might have been frozen before we found you."

Floyd's teeth chattered as he tried to speak. "I couldn't see the road, and a truck came barreling at us around that curve. My car won't start. We need to get home. Our parents will be worried."

"Frantic, is what I heard," the trooper said. "We've sent another cruiser ahead to the station. They'll call your parents to let them know we've found you."

"How are we going to get home?" Willa asked, hunched in a knot and trying to rub some life into her numb hands.

"Probably put you on a bus," the trooper said. "You can call your parents yourselves when you get to the station."

A second trooper, damp from trekking down into the ravine, opened the passenger door and jumped into the cruiser. He removed his wide-brimmed hat and shook the water into the footwell between his booted feet. "You guys okay?" he asked, tossing the words into the back seat, too cold and stiff to turn his head. "Let's get them to the station," he said to his partner. Turning slightly toward the back seat as the cruiser pulled away from the shoulder he said to Floyd, "Did a job on that guard rail."

Standing beside the empty desk in the warm police station, Floyd's face expressed confusion as he listened to his father when the operator got him on the phone.

"Yes, Father," Floyd said. "I understand. No, Father. Nothing happened. We had an accident."

When Willa and Floyd stepped down from the idling Greyhound bus in Clairdale, both fathers were at the station to meet them. Instead of being thrilled at their children's safe return, both fathers were angry and gruff.

"I don't know what you two were thinking," Stewart Miller said as he watched his daughter climb into the back seat of Blain Keller's car. "Out all night alone. It's nearly killed your mothers."

"You've shamed us in front of the whole church," Floyd's father said, repeating himself for the third time.

"I don't understand—" Floyd began.

"Silence," Blain Keller boomed as he started the car. "We'll discuss it when we get home."

Both families had gathered at Floyd's home to await the arrival of their children. It felt like walking the plank as Willa and Floyd, followed by their fathers, walked up the wide front steps, across the wet porch and into the dark front parlor that smelled like furniture polish and old leather. Panic, mixed with pain filled the mothers' eyes as they hugged and kissed their children, stood back to inspect them for minor cuts and bruises, then unleashed their condemnations.

"Shamed us in front of the church," Annabelle Keller whimpered. "We won't be able to show our faces ever again." She shot a guilt-laden look toward Floyd. "It's our whole life destroyed. First your sister, now you."

"Shamed us in front of the whole world," Hetty Miller cried, dabbing at her red nose with a crumpled handkerchief. "I've had heart palpitations since Blain called the police."

Willa's mother took a deep breath and lifted her head to face

Willa. "Your purity has been defiled. No good man will ever want you. What will we do? We'll be stuck with you forever."

"They will get married, like we discussed," Blain Keller said. He glared at every person in the shadowy room, demanding silent agreement. "Isn't that what we agreed?" He took a seat and ordered the others to do the same.

"What?" Floyd cried, turning frantically from one adult to the other, his mouth hanging open in utter disbelief. Since descending the slippery bus steps, he had not been allowed to speak more than a few short denials to their awful accusations. Refusing to sit, he bent forward in a beseeching attitude and said, "I don't want to get married yet, and I don't want to marry Willa. I hardly know her. I want to pick my own wife, court her and fall in love with her."

"Sit down," Blain said.

Floyd dropped into a stiff chair but kept his back straight and his head up, hiding his fear and agony behind a glassy-eyed stare that still held some remnant of hope.

"All the niceties of courtship you are so attached to," Hetty Miller said, "went out the window when you two spent the night together in a car, alone, on some back road in Kentucky. If we're ever going to face our friends and neighbors again, it must be with the announcement of the marriage of our daughter. Her spotless reputation must be protected."

Willa gasped. Tears filled her eyes. She didn't know whether to be shocked, angry, or delirious with happiness. All she'd dared hope for was some conversation on the ride home, and maybe, in the future, at church, a little acknowledgment from Floyd that she was alive. She looked at the tortured faces locked on Floyd and her.

"Married?" Willa said in a soft voice of surprise. "Me?"

"Don't play the innocent with us," Floyd's mother said. "Who knows what you two have done, cuddled together, alone in the woods."

"Father," Floyd began, employing the rational and persuasive tone of conciliation he was developing for use in his profession, "I understand that you all are upset, but it was an accident." For the first time since they'd reached home, Floyd's father let him finish two sentences. "A truck came barreling around a corner and drove us off the road. We were trapped in the car in a ravine, out of sight. If you hadn't called the police and asked them to search for us, we'd probably still be there. I'm sure the police told you they had to break us out of the car. We nearly froze to death." His eyes searched the faces of his father and mother, pleading for understanding and forgiveness. "You know I want to choose my own wife and that I have committed to finishing seminary first. Please don't make that choice for me."

Blain Keller stood up as though he were preparing to make a speech. "Are you through?" he asked. "Because I'm going to say this just once and then it's settled." He ran his fingers through his thick gray hair, released a deep breath and dropped heavily back onto the worn couch in the deathly quiet living room. Only the staccato ticking of a mantel clock penetrated the silence. Blain exchanged a brief look with his wife, as though sealing an agreement they'd made. Then he looked straight into Floyd's eyes and spoke. "When you had rheumatic fever—you were about twelve—I promised that if the Lord would save your life and let you grow into manhood, healthy and strong, that I would dedicate you to his service." Floyd's mother reached over and took her husband's hand, a look of pain and conviction forcing her lips into a thin hard line.

"When your sister died of scarlet fever, after God had spared you, I knew his message was clear: he wanted you and needed you in his service." Floyd's father paused and looked around at the others then returned his hard glare to Floyd. "You cannot serve our Lord with a cloud of sexual misconduct hanging over your head. You will never be ordained into the ministry unless you make a respectable woman out of Willa and embrace her as your wife in Christ. Only through an expeditious marriage can you hope to undo the damage you have done to your reputation and salvage your ministry for your Savior. He died on the cross for your sins. It is the least you can do for him."

Floyd's feelings could not have been more obvious as his shoulders slumped forward, his hands fell limp between his knees, and his eyes vacantly traced the dull pattern on the carpet. He aged before his family's eyes as the vitality of youth seeped from his bones and he acquiesced to his fate.

Willa watched him through hooded eyes. She understood there was nothing that would change his father's decision and she knew Floyd could not go back on his commitment to God.

Floyd didn't look at Willa to see how she felt, but she knew, oh yes, she was clear about how she felt.

Not one outward sign revealed her feelings as she maintained her rigid pose and let her inner passions run wild. She could see that Floyd was sad, perhaps even angry. He certainly didn't love her. But she would love Floyd, more than life itself. She would finish college and be the best minister's wife on the face of the earth. She would bear his children, clean his house, cook his meals, and throw her body in front of a speeding train, if required. The vague idea of dying for Floyd gave her a giddy feeling. She would play the organ in his church and set an example to the congregation of how a righteous wife served God. A chill of ecstasy passed through her tired body. She clasped her hands in her lap and shuddered as a warm flow of pleasure tingled in her private parts and a gush of joy permeated her groin.

In the days that followed, Floyd and Willa were feted at church celebrations and dragged into counseling sessions with parents and elders of the church. They were lectured on the responsibilities of marriage and raising a family though not once was the topic of sex discussed.

The ladies of the church's Charity Society gathered at Willa's house every afternoon to alter her mother's wedding gown and assemble a makeshift trousseau.

"Shorten the bodice; she's short-waisted," one advised.

"Let out the waistline two inches; it shows that little roll around her middle," another instructed.

They poked her with pins, mussed her hair and fussed with the droop of her breasts. "You can tell she isn't my natural child," her mother announced. "Look at that posture."

Yes, Willa said to herself, you can tell I'm not your natural child; you remind me daily.

Willa was her mother's niece, formally adopted by her aunt and uncle when she'd been an infant and her parents had died in a flood.

"We wanted to do the right thing," her adopted mother had told her since she was old enough to understand. "God acts in mysterious ways. Your father and I believe that though we didn't want to have children of our own, my health being so frail and all, that we should take you in and give you a good Christian upbringing." She would pat Willa's tiny shoulder and add, "We must serve the Lord in whatever capacity he offers, though it may be burdensome."

The wedding took place in the sanctuary on December 29th with a reception following in the function room in the church basement. Willa, a proverbial wallflower, found herself basking in the limelight as the other young women in the church showered her with attention and placed her center stage, a new bride and the envy of all of them.

Though the church forbade drinking, smoking and dancing, the reception was a happy and joyous event as a rare opportunity for celebration was always welcome in their somber lives.

"Just think!" Willa was saying to a college classmate. "When I return to college, I'll be an old married lady. I'll know things those girls have only dreamed about."

"You're not returning to college," her mother said, appearing suddenly at her elbow. "What makes you think we're sending you back now?"

Willa whirled around in her chair, disbelief in her eyes. "What did you say, Mother?" she asked. Blood pounded in her ears. A searing pain crashed from temple to temple. Education was her life! A dream of teaching music had been her beacon of hope all her young years. Music was her passion, classical music, religious music, the music of angels and heaven! She held her breath.

"I said, your father and I are not sending you back to college. I assumed you knew that. You have a husband now. You're his responsibility." Hetty Miller stopped a moment to take in the shock on her daughter's face. She changed her calloused tone to sound more reasonable. "You are perfectly well prepared to be a minister's wife. You play the organ beautifully and you have a good basic education. You don't need a bachelor's degree to wife." She gave a smug grin to Annabelle who was obviously listening in. "It's time you stayed home and learned the arts of homemaking."

Willa gasped and clutched her hands to her chest. Tears burst forth from her eyes like fountains and streamed down her reddened cheeks. What little beauty her wedding day had brought out in her plain face, faded as the final details of her fate were revealed to her.

"You will go to live with the Kellers and Annabelle will complete your training as a housewife." Hetty looked over at Annabelle; they exchanged nods of agreement. "You know how hard it has been for me to teach you the basics, what with my frail health and all."

Willa jumped to her feet, tripping over the flared skirt of her yellowed but precious wedding gown and fled toward the exit.

Hetty signaled for Annabelle to join her as she followed close on Willa's heels. "I can't see for the life of me what is the matter with that girl," she called over her shoulder to Annabelle. "Must be bride's nerves. Girls," she said as Annabelle caught up and took her arm. "Foolish and selfish."

"And on the happiest day of her life," Annabelle said.

Chapter 6

Be Fruitful and Multiply

In addition to her household chores, helping with the cooking and laundry, and sitting through meetings in church, Willa practiced her music. She resumed piano and organ lessons with her local teacher and prayed every night that she could find contentment with her new life.

"I don't mean to complain, Dear Jesus, but it is so lonely sleeping in Floyd's old bedroom while he's away at school," she prayed at night. "Please forgive me for my sins of greed and selfishness, but I did believe that if I got married we would be together." Willa paused her bedside prayer to wipe away tears that came every night of their own accord.

Annabelle treated her with Christian kindness, but like her adopted mother, her mother-in-law never put her arm around her. No one ever hugged Willa.

Even when Floyd had finally consummated their marriage, he had performed with a level of chastity that left Willa feeling she had become a nun, not a wife. After intercourse that first night, she had changed the bloody sheets and crawled back into bed and rolled over next to Floyd to be held and cuddled. That's what happened in the few romance novels she had sneaked home from friends and read secretly at night.

***

Floyd didn't cuddle her that night nor during the nights that followed. When he'd left for school, he'd given her a formal kiss on the cheek and hurried out the door.

On April Fool's Day morning, Willa didn't come down to fix breakfast. When Annabelle entered her bedroom to wake her, she spied the enamel pail next to Willa's bed.

"What's the matter with you?" Annabelle asked. "You haven't started breakfast. Are you sick?"

"I've been throwing up," Willa said from her pillow.

"That's not funny," Annabelle said. "Floyd was always quick with the April Fool's jokes. I'm sure he put you up to this. Get dressed and come downstairs right away. I'll start the oatmeal."

"I can't, Mrs. Keller," Willa said. "I'm sick. I feel awful."

Annabelle went over, brushed aside Willa's scraggly straight bangs, and felt Willa's damp forehead. "You don't feel sick to me. I'll see you downstairs." She turned away and left the room, closing the door behind her. Suddenly she burst back through the door and cried, "You're not! Oh good lord! You can't be!" She came closer and peered down at Willa's pale face and matted hair. "You're pregnant!"

Annabelle headed out the door again yelling, "Blain! Blain! Come here at once!" She met her frightened husband halfway down the stairs and dragged him into the room now shared by Floyd and Willa. Terrified by Annabelle's shrill cries, Willa had sat up and pulled the bedclothes up to cover her nightgown.

"She's what?" Blain cried as Annabelle dragged him into the bedroom and pulled him close to the bed.

"She's pregnant, Blain!" Annabelle pointed at the enamel bucket and then at Willa. "She's going to have a baby!"

"How could that be?" he cried in confusion. "Floyd is in school. He has more than two years to go before he can support a family." He looked at his wife's flushed face and slowly came to his senses. He turned to Willa and said more gently, "I'm sorry. I just didn't think things happened that fast. Annabelle and I took more care and planned our children when we could afford them."

Willa buried her face in the sheet and blanket tented over her

47

knees. "I'm sorry," she said in a muffled voice. "I didn't mean it to happen so quickly."

"Only the good lord knows the truth in that statement." Annabelle grasped her husband's arm again and dragged him out into the hall. She shut Willa's door behind them. Willa could hear their lowered voices as they descended the stairs together muttering over her newest crime.

When Willa finally came downstairs, washed and dressed, she found Hetty sitting at the kitchen table in hushed conversation with Annabelle.

"Good morning, Mother," Willa said as she went to the Frigidaire for a glass of tomato juice.

"Thank the good lord you got married," her mother said. "No one will ever be able to argue about a week or two."

Willa sat down and let out a painful sigh. She looked at her mother and then at Annabelle and said quietly, speaking in a slow cadence even a child could understand, "Floyd and I did not have physical relations until after we were married. I'll swear that on a stack of Bibles."

"Don't talk like that in my house!" Annabelle admonished. "You mustn't take the Lord's name in vain."

"I might just have the flu," Willa said. "Perhaps I should go see the doctor."

"I most certainly hope you will," Hetty said. "You don't want to upset Floyd about burdening him with a child if you only have the flu."

***

Floyd couldn't afford to come home for Spring break, what with the cost of repairs to his car and all. He placed a few dutiful phone calls to Willa and finally headed home at the end of the semester in late May. But his feelings on the drive back to Clairdale were different from past trips. Instead of watching the miles whiz past while he listened to the radio and anticipated his mother's home cooking and his own cozy room, his thoughts ran to darkness, resentment at his situation and a disturbing anger toward god.

Though he knew that sorrow and hardship befell God's lambs, victims of life's troubles whom he was being groomed to tend, he'd assumed his life would be one of peace and comfort, filled with the tender caring of God's flock but safe in the knowledge that he had been chosen and would be protected. Now he wondered who cared for the shepherd. Was he to live the life of Job, once blessed and contented and now assaulted by plagues and misery?

He opened his car window to the gentle May breeze and spit, a new and irritating habit he'd formed since his marriage. It felt like bile was rising up from his stomach and there was no place to store it. When he couldn't spit out the venomous bile, he swallowed and retained his bitterness in a small pocket of suffused rage that ate at his heart like battery acid. He banged his fist on the steering wheel as he drove along the mountain valley where he and Willa had spent that awful night in the car. As the bent and twisted guardrail, symbolic of his derailed life, came into view, he slowed and pulled over. He stopped the car and spit out the window again. He gazed down into the scrub-covered gully and longed to turn back the clock, to feel that ray of sunshine inside him that he'd felt had been put there by the Lord. But that ray of light had been banished, replaced by blackness like the open mouth of a coal mine. Instead of joyful anticipation for each day that had been his former life, he now felt like he was lost in the bowels of that abandoned mine and had taken so many wrong turns he would never emerge alive.

Floyd pulled his gaze away from the crumpled guardrail and stared forward. Waiting for him at home was his summer job in the warehouse of his father's furniture store and a wife he loathed. But his fate was sealed; it must be God's will.

As he'd done since his marriage to Willa, Floyd tried to stop his negative ruminations and turn his thoughts to the power of God's love. Surely, he reminded himself for the thousandth time, the Lord would give him no burden greater than he could bear. When he got home, he would see Willa differently. He would not focus on her pasty skin, her lumpy buttocks and her protruding front teeth. He would look on her as one of God's flock, his helpmate, and the person that God had chosen for his future.

But his sacrificed romantic dreams continued their battle with his pragmatic thoughts as he clenched his jaw, depressed the clutch pedal, and shifted into gear.

He felt exhausted as he pulled back onto the highway, like Jacob wrestling with the angel in the night. Again, as he counted the flashing white lines in the center of the road, he wondered if the dawn would ever come as it had for Jacob. Would Floyd ever feel blessed by the Lord again?

***

At home Floyd made no comments about Willa's increased girth. When others were present, Floyd treated Willa in a courteous manner, rising from the table to fetch a glass of water, or assisting her with her car door. In private, he seemed preoccupied, barely acknowledging her presence. When they were alone together, he kept his nose buried in a book, boning up for the next semester, he told her.

Most evenings the family gathered on the front porch to read, play board games and listen to the latest war news on the radio. Kaiser Wilhelm II had died; Germany was now declaring war on the Soviet Union, and all of Europe was in turmoil.

Many evenings were spent at the church for meetings and special gatherings. Sabbaths, as always, started with Sabbath school, followed by church services. Often church was followed by picnics or trips to the state park for walks along the lovely woodland trails or the study of flowers and birds.

Despite Willa's efforts to face reality, she was disappointed that she didn't have to fend off Floyd's sexual advances as the fetus grew. He said he wanted to be a considerate husband and would not impose himself on her in her advanced condition. His words sounded kind but lacked conviction. In truth, Willa had longed for him to return for the summer. Deep inside, as ugly as her thoughts might be, she longed for him to impose himself on her. She was eager to be ravished.

She'd been fatigued after the Fourth of July picnic and had needed to lie down, asking Floyd if he cared to join her for a nap.

"You go ahead and rest," he'd said as he headed outside to the front porch and the metal glider. "I've got some reading I want to finish."

Alone in their bedroom overlooking the roof of the back porch, Willa removed her thin summer dress and damp slip and tugged a nightgown over her protruding abdomen. She pulled her eyes away from the linea nigra that was spreading down her midline, marveling at how ugly the body grew during pregnancy. She lay down in the still air, longing for a breeze at the window, but none came. As the sun dropped down over the line of trees in the backyard, she wept.

It's a sin, she told herself. I know I must be an evil woman, but I want Floyd to touch me and love me. She ran her hand down over her belly then pulled up her gown to touch her dark pubic hair she could no longer see without a mirror. What kind of evil woman am I to hunger for his touch? Maybe he knows without any words that I am depraved, and he is trying to help heal me. He must know best; he is a man of God. He is my husband. I must submit to his will.

She heard movement and low voices below on the back porch. The sound of scraping on wood rose from the rockers as chairs were shifted around. "If you could say she'd ever been pretty," Annabelle said to an unidentified friend. "She's sure lost her looks."

"Most women have a glow when they're pregnant," the friend said. "My daughter looked like someone had turned on the sunshine wherever she went."

"She was pretty to start," Annabelle said. "Oh, I know it is unchristian of me to complain, but I had pictured Floyd, so handsome, married to a tall and lovely woman, modest and devoted." The screen door slammed.

"You ladies gossiping?" Floyd asked. Willa could picture his flashing devilish grin. "You know gossip is naughty." She'd seen him tease his mother's friends and watched as they blushed like shy young maidens.

"Oh, Floyd," the friend said with a giggle. "You're such a tease. No one can resist you. Eager to return to the seminary?"

"Yes," he said. "I miss my studies. Recovery is so lovely, I find myself spiritually uplifted just being there and devoting my attentions to my courses."

Willa didn't go down for supper that night. She cried herself to sleep.

***

Floyd came home when Enoch was born near the end of September 1941, but hurried back to school, anxious about missing too many classes.

"You be a good mother and give him all your love," Floyd said as he kissed the baby good-bye and gave Willa a dutiful peck on her sunken cheek. "You take good care of your mother," he said to little Enoch as he jumped into his car and spun gravel backing out of the driveway.

By the time Floyd graduated from the seminary, was ordained, and then posted to the position of assistant pastor and youth leader in the Cleveland, Ohio church, the United States was deeply embroiled in the Second World War.

Within the confines of a church community, somewhat like the confines of a cloister, the effects of world shattering events can be muted. Floyd, Willa and Enoch lived a quiet life. Floyd ministered to the congregation and ran youth programs, though the ranks of young men had thinned considerably. Most charity activities in the church devoted their efforts to the war in addition to their support for the poor and needy in their local community.

Families, bowed by sadness over the loss of fathers and sons, leaned more heavily on their faith in God to help them through the dark times. Most young men who were members of the Circle of Redemption of the World served their country as conscientious objectors. But death took its toll of these gentle souls along with the rank and file.

Willa tended to their small home and took delight in baby Enoch, the joy of her life. She loved him as she'd never been able to love anyone else before and he returned her devotion with toothless smiles and bubbles of drool. She filled in at church as assistant organist and played many evenings for choir practice. She kept a neat home and found that without the critical supervision of Annabelle, she enjoyed her time in the kitchen and developed into a respectable cook.

Deprived of all the extras and finding most basics in short supply, Willa contented herself with simple meals while starting a tiny collection of cheap specialty dishes for her glass-fronted cupboard in the dining room. She poked around in junk shops for salad bowls shaped like lettuce leaves, small corn boats that looked like concave ears of corn and an old soup tureen that looked more like a goiter gone wild than the bloated beet it represented.

***

Like a special Christmas present—to make up for his general indifference, Willa guessed—Floyd made love to her. On September 28, 1944, three years less one day after Enoch's birth, Rachel was born.

Rachel was a blond baby with opaque blue eyes that eventually turned green, and a smile that brought light and warmth to the quiet house. Willa would kiss her cherub and put her down to nap, then pick up little Enoch and spend hours with him, consumed by the need to give the unlimited love to her babies that she'd never had. To Willa's surprise and joy, Floyd took more interest in Rachel as an infant than he had in Enoch. Probably because he's home with us and not worried about his studies and examinations, she told herself.

The double bed that Willa and Floyd shared was more than ample for the undisturbed sleep of two sprawling adults, but Floyd had mastered sleeping on the edge. A modicum of warmth seeped into their marriage though sexual activity was rare and tentative. Willa thanked God for the crumbs of affection Floyd tossed her way and felt less of a need to weep in the middle of the night.

When the war ended, the world breathed a collective sigh of relief and went about rebuilding nation after destroyed nation. Men came home from the war; congregations swelled; and babies were born in a monster wave. The pall of so much death and maiming was forced into the shadows by the lusty cries of so many new lives.

In 1946, Floyd received his first posting to a church as its head minister, independent of supervision and trusted with the needs and souls of a whole congregation. Floyd moved his family to Buffalo, New York where he became responsible not only for the church but the church school, a junior academy including grades one through ten. With all the love of God in his heart and his deep commitment to serving the Lord, Floyd took on his responsibilities with fervid energy.

Willa cared for the home and their children and played the organ every Sabbath, sitting ramrod straight on the high organ bench, gliding her hands smoothly over the keys while her short legs moved in frantic thrusts so her toes could press the foot pedals. Between songs, she took her seat in the front row and tended to her babies while she gazed lovingly up at her husband as he preached.

Floyd was the sword and shield of God, leading, preaching, helping and healing the parishioners. Willa was his help-meet, the shining example to the congregation of how a godly woman lived and raised a family and loved her husband. When she sat in the front pew, listening to her husband's inspired words, she could feel the eyes of the church members as they moved from Floyd to her and back to Floyd, always watching, always weighing, always aware if she made a slip.

Every word out of Willa's mouth was either monitored by Floyd or advised in advance.

"Remember, we are God's servants," Floyd would admonish her. "We are the living example to those who are looking to learn. Our children must sit still during services. If they make a peep, take them outside the sanctuary until you have better control over them. Don't be afraid to spank Enoch for squirming." He'd follow his instructions with his standard order, an order that Willa secretly refused to obey. "Make sure he kisses your hand after you spank him. He needs to show affection to he who chastises him, whether chastisement comes from the Lord, you, or me."

Before any church event: celebrations, picnics, vespers, or home visits, Floyd always admonished Willa. "Now remember, every word out of your mouth, every glance will be judged. Never can you be caught short of brotherly love and acceptance for even the most slovenly backslider. We are God's servants. We must carry out his will."

***

Willa tried to be perfect, but by 1950 when Jessie was born and left her stillborn twin behind, Willa had begun to fray at the edges. She gave her children all the love she could give, but there was none for her from the man she quite literally worshiped.

For the first six months after her birth, Jessie was colicky and didn't sleep through the night. Willa spent hours rocking her baby and pacing the floors, frantic the infant's cries would keep Floyd awake.

As the stresses of raising a family increased his daily burdens, Floyd became irritable and more distant, dispensing stormy looks and harsh words to Willa over breakfast. In a flare of temper he would strike her, keeping his blows within the hairline where a bruise would heal undetected. "Now, kiss my hand," he would demand afterward. "Remember, it is the Lord who striketh you and it is He who chasteneth you for your sinful ways."

A thundercloud seemed to hover over Floyd at home as Rachel's face slowly became disfigured. A progressive thyroid disease caused her eyes to bulge, puzzling the doctors and erasing little Rachel's beauty.

Enoch's calm and sweet soul had provided a small island of love and warmth in Willa's daily existence. She wept with loneliness when Enoch went off to school. Her heart ached as she watched him struggle with his p's and q's; he tried so hard. When Enoch was held back in the first grade she knew that Floyd would blame her. "How can he become a minister," Floyd railed at Willa, "if he's too stupid to read? First you lose Jessie's twin, then Rachel is disfigured with a horrible disease, and now Enoch can't read. Looks to me like all you can bear is damaged children."

After his most outrageous cruelties, Floyd would drive away in his car—to visit a sick person, he'd often tell Willa—and return a few hours later with a bouquet of flowers or maybe a cheap box of chocolates. Though he never expressed words of love, nor ever tossed out a few crumbs of apology, he would leave his token of regret in the kitchen or put the candy on her pillow.

Like snow in July, Willa's heart always melted and she'd remind herself that things would be better. All she had to do was show forgiveness, seventy times seven as it said in the Bible. She'd remind herself that outside their home, Floyd was sunny and pleasant, devoted to his flock. There wasn't a woman in the congregation who didn't admire him. Sometimes she thought they envied her and would trade places with her if they could, every one of them. What she really needed to do, she'd chide herself, was cheer up, forget the pain, and see Floyd in a better light.

CHAPTER 7

Homework

The Shyler, Massachusetts police station was showing signs of decay, rotting from the inside. Townsfolk driving by the trim single-story brick building could see no reason for the push to build a new, larger facility. But then, most Shyler residents were law-abiding citizens and had never been inside the cramped rooms, or seen the halls with stained and threadbare carpets, or sat in the tiny offices where dented file cabinets lined sagging walls and files and boxes were stacked to the ceilings in threatening heaps.

In the one interrogation room, leaks from the flat roof had created works of uncertain art in the yellowed fiberglass ceiling tiles. At the beginning of the interview with Jessie Keller, Detective Joe D'nardo had pointed to the brown watermarks on the ceiling, suggesting they were Rorschach tests in the formative stage. "Perhaps you can interpret them for me," he'd said with a grin. Half an hour later, he sat leaning back in a metal chair glancing at the ceiling while obviously creating a strategic silence between them.

"You say Butch physically abused Rachel?" Joe asked again.

"Yes," Jessie said.

Three days had passed since the death of Butch Vogel. Under indictment, Jessie had been given a week off from work to sort things out. In the past three nights, free of her newspaper reporting duties, Jessie had slept more than she'd slept since she'd been a teenager, excepting her night in the holding cell, of course. She snuffed her cigarette out in the ash-encrusted tin ashtray. She tapped her left foot nervously under the metal interrogation table and clicked her fingernails on the scuffed surface. Sitting still had always been hard for Jessie. She could still recall being smacked for squirming in her seat in church. Now, rested and bored, having to sit in this dull gray room with the barred window was making her skin crawl.

"I've searched the police records," Joe said. "I went back ten years, to the day they were married. Nothing." He gazed steadily into Jessie's dark brown eyes. Jessie could tell Joe enjoyed looking at her; most men did. She responded with a faint smile. "There is no record of domestic problems," he said.

"Police don't report abuse in their own families." She said it simply, looking directly into Joe's eyes.

Joe opened his mouth to respond, thought a moment, then said, "You're right and you're wrong. It may not get reported, for the records, but it does get handled. This is an officer's sister whom you say was being abused. I assume you know that police generally take care of their own. Don't you think if Rachel had reported a beating that Butch would have received a little reminder to not do it again?" Joe offered a wry grin and referred to his notes. "Plus, as you know, your brother has only been on the force the past four years and there is nothing prior."

"What percent of domestic abuse incidents get reported at all?" Jessie asked.

"Obviously I don't know but I'd guess under twenty percent. Let's face it, it's not uncommon, unfortunately." Joe flipped a page in his notebook.

"The fingerprints on the alleged murder weapon are yours but neither that pan, nor any of the others have Rachel's fingerprints on them. Can you explain that to me?"

"Cleanliness is next to Godliness."

"Perhaps you could be a little less cryptic."

"Rachel is fastidious. Not only does she keep her house spotless, she likes cooking. She loved that baker's rack of shining pots and pans. Said it gave a homey glow to her kitchen."

"That doesn't explain no fingerprints."

"When Rachel washed her copper pots, she finished them with a solution of vinegar and coarse salt. Then she rinsed them and dried them with towels, never letting her fingers touch the surfaces as she restored them to their place on the rack. Every pot had a place. She was religious about that." Jessie cradled her large purse in her lap and tapped nervously on the dull leather. "That's the best explanation I can give." She looked at the door with a twinge of longing for escape. "Actually," she said, looking back at Joe, "I'd never thought about it before."

"Thank you for stopping by," Joe said, rising and heading for the door. "When is Butch's funeral?"

"In an hour."

Joe squinted his eyes as he twisted the metal knob and pulled the heavy door open for Jessie. "I'm puzzled by this whole thing," he said. "Something's bugging me."

"With a glass eye and a soiled raincoat," Jessie said, "you could be Colombo."

Joe grinned and stepped out into the hallway behind Jessie. "When the funeral's over this afternoon, would you come back to the station and talk with me?"

"Why should I want to talk to a cop?" Jessie asked. "I've confessed twice, given you a written statement, and spent half my life savings to retain the best lawyer in Boston to make sure you get the facts right. I accidentally snuffed out the lights of an abusive bastard who was trying to kill my sister." She pawed through her purse for her car keys. "You want me to stand trial for manslaughter when you should be glad the son-of-a-bitch is dead."

At the main entrance to the station, Joe reached around Jessie to push the door open for her.

"I need your help," he said.

59

***

Behind Jessie's veil of black, worn only to comply with her mother's commitment to social conventions, Jessie wore the faintest trace of a smile as she watched Enoch do double-duty. Choosing to wear his Sabbath suit rather than his uniform, he'd assigned himself two difficult tasks: supporting Willa, and shielding Jessie.

As members of the congregation thronged through the Kellers' home after observing Butch's burial, it was evident they struggled with their Christian mandate to forgive seven times seven. Offering condolences to Willa and Floyd came easily and flowed gently in subdued voices. Their remarks to Jessie, a backslider, who no longer attended the Fenwell church, were more awkward. They hardened their hearts toward this young woman who preyed on the misfortunes of others and who had allegedly killed her brother-in-law. They sniffed the air as they passed her. She must know they could detect the smell of cigarette smoke on her clothes. Who was she kidding?

Jessie did her best to hide her cynical smile as she watched the guests sample the simple foods piled on the large dining room table. Balancing tasty morsels on thin paper plates, they wandered through the kitchen and out into the sun porch of her parents' 1950s ranch home. She saw them taking in the details of the carved music rack on the familiar organ in the living room. When Floyd had retired from the Fenwell church and taken a position as Vice President of Publications and Communications at the conference headquarters, the church had replaced the organ in the sanctuary, giving this older and much smaller instrument to their dear Pastor Keller as a small token of their esteem and gratitude for the six years he'd ministered to their needs.

By the time her father had left his role as an active minister, a deep rift had been carved between Floyd and his younger daughter Jessie. Choosing to pursue journalism at a large Boston university rather than attending Recovery University or one of the religion's sister schools had been insult enough to Floyd. To have to shell out his hard-earned cash for a college where he couldn't get any financial assistance and where his daughter could pursue her career in the exploitation of other peoples' misfortunes had put him further at odds with Jessie. He had warned her repeatedly that she would come to no good.

After her first year in college, Jessie had insisted she could no longer commute to Boston; it depleted her energy for school. She'd moved into a student apartment near her school in 1969 and had never resided in this house on the edge of Fenwell where her parents had moved in mid 1970.

"How are you holding up?" Enoch asked Jessie, returning to her side as though his presence could protect her from unkind stares. "Mother is fading fast."

"I'm fine," Jessie said, surveying the punch bowl and the wilting orange slices floating on the cranberry mixture. "Too bad we aren't Irish. At least I could get a stiff drink."

Enoch gave her shoulders a brief squeeze.

"Rather dry for the likes of you," he said softly. "You staying for supper? There are enough casseroles and pies to feed us for a month."

"D'nardo asked me to come by the station when this was over. I haven't decided what I'll do yet. I was hoping to fit in a visit with Rachel but Mother says she is still unresponsive."

"I went to see her yesterday," Enoch said. "It's like someone flipped a switch and the lights went out."

***

Jessie tugged the sleeve of Enoch's suit jacket leading him through the living room and back into the hallway that ran along the far end of the house where the three bedrooms were located. "I need to talk to you," she said as she dragged him into their father's study and closed the door. She sat on the edge of a small couch, pushing some papers aside and dropping her purse to the floor. "Why would D'nardo want to talk to me again?"

"I'm not sure," Enoch said, pulling the chair out from his father's desk and sitting down. "He's been asking me a lot of questions too, questions about you, Rachel, Butch, you know, doing his homework."

"Well I'm not his special assignment," Jessie said leaning back on the couch. "I didn't mean to kill that piece of shit but he's dead. It was accidental. I don't get why the cops can't see that. For Christ sakes! Getting killed accidentally doesn't stop the presses. It happens every day."

"I agree with you," Enoch said. "Remember, I'm on the front lines now." He toyed with a small pile of paper clips next to his father's worn Bible. Picking up the Bible, he pushed the chair further back and spun around to face Jessie. "Funny," he said. "I can't remember seeing our father without this Bible in his hands."

"Me neither," Jessie said. "Why do you think he still takes it everywhere? He's not even a minister any more." Jessie paused and asked, "Did you always carry a Bible when you were a minister?"

"No," Enoch said. He laid the Bible back on the desk and turned back to Jessie. "Regarding your question about D'nardo, I may have an answer. I just hope it's not affecting the way he handles your case."

"Tell me," Jessie said.

Enoch looked at her and frowned. "This is strictly off the record, dear sister. Off the record."

"Off the record," she confirmed with a smile.

"Our chief and the DA think that Joe is concerned with proving himself here in Shyler. Everyone knows why Joe left Springfield."

"What are you talking about? He's new to Shyler?"

"Hasn't been here six months."

"Go on," Jessie prompted.

"Detective D'nardo was the head Crime Scene Investigator on

the Springfield Police force. He was younger than most of his peers but he was bright and aggressive. He never assumed anything and cleared more cases in his five years as chief detective than they'd closed in the prior decade."

"Why'd he leave Springfield? From what I know, most cops grow up and serve in their home town."

"D'nardo is a cop's cop, for sure, but first and foremost, he's an honest cop," Enoch continued. "He was in a position that I think about sometimes when I can't sleep at night. He was in the wrong place at the wrong time and saw one of his closest friends take a bribe. His friend had been on the take for a long time, just never had been found out."

"D'nardo didn't have to rat him out."

"He was already under investigation. The way Springfield Internal Affairs went after Joe, he had no choice. And it cost him everything."

"Cops don't get fired for telling the truth," Jessie said. Her tone became scornful. "Though I've seen cops I was convinced didn't know the difference. For Christ sakes, I've seen cops lie on the witness stand as coolly as they order a free cup of coffee and a glazed donut."

"He didn't get fired. It was much worse for him."

"How do you know all of this if it happened in Springfield? That's on the other side of the state."

"We're a nosey bunch," Enoch said with a grin. "We do our homework." He started to rise from his chair. "We like to get the background story, just like you."

"Sit down," Jessie said. "I don't accept half stories."

Enoch dropped back into his father's chair and focused his attention on the small cluster of pictures on the wall over Rachel's head. Birds, all the colorful birds he remembered from his father's battered bird book: goldfinch, painted bunting, rose-breasted grosbeak and the obnoxious blue jay. Birdhouses. He shook his head to clear the memories and resumed his story.

"Joe was married to the daughter of a retired captain. You know, a police brat. She and Joe never had any children but he was very happy. His wife handled the role of a policeman's wife well, having grown up in that environment, never complaining at his irregular hours, always keeping a brave face on it, and happy when he got home. He had it good."

"They're not married any more?"

"That was the price he paid for being honest. It's a tight fraternity, Jessie, a social community, a lot like life on a military base. When a cop gets hurt or killed, his police family is there for him. Everyone knows everyone else." Enoch noted Jessie's bored expression. "I'm sorry. I forget you learn all this stuff doing your job." He picked at the crease in his slacks. "This is too hot for July.

"Like any family, a police family can turn away from you. The story goes that Joe's wife suffered from the loss of community that developed after Joe testified against his buddy. Joe was shunned at work but took that in stride. He knew most of the guys that made cutting remarks in public agreed with his actions in private. He understood how they felt and accepted his ostracization as par for the course. In time, they'd get over it and he could wait. Word is he loved his job and was the best detective in the 413 area code."

"So."

"Joe was toughing it out, though I guess things were getting pretty bad at home. One day in the ready room, one of the guys made a remark about an officer enjoying the fruits of Joe's training. Joe didn't take his meaning until another guy said, 'No use breaking in your own mare when you can get one that's already saddle broken and never balks.'

"Turns out that Joe's wife was sleeping with one of the SWAT guys. By the time Joe caught on and confronted her, she was so done with Joe that she admitted to the affair and said she wanted a divorce."

"Wow," Jessie said. "That is a high price to pay. Wish I'd had that story." Suddenly she bent forward, yanked her notebook from her purse and began writing.

"What are you writing?" Enoch asked.

"Nothing." She wrote fast and furiously in that abbreviated scrawl she called Jessie-scratch.

"Remember, Jessie. What I just told you is off the record."

Enoch looked at his little sister whose penchant to report on other people's pain continued to surprise him. He knew she was achieving success in the Boston media scene, but he often winced at her delight in doing whatever it took to get the story. He knew local reporters like her. For twenty-six, she was well on the way to growing the barnacles of a hard drinking, passionately driven sleuth who would gladly step over dead bodies to get the real story. Capable for sure, he would gladly acknowledge, but a bit overconfident in his opinion.

He looked at her open expression, her full mouth, her fashionable hairstyle, her trim, petite figure and her ubiquitous gold hoops. (She said they symbolized her walk on the wild side, her Gypsy soul.) Though they were nine years apart, and he'd played a very small role as older brother in her younger years, he liked her. He liked her spunk. He liked her ability to think for herself and her guts in standing up to their father. He smiled when the memory of her phrase "the evil twin" flitted through his mind. I've totally forgotten about that, he said to himself as he watched her write. Her twin had been stillborn. When Jessie was in fifth grade, she'd written a story about the twin whose strength she'd robbed so she could live. That had set their quiet home into an uproar, he recalled. It had overshadowed his graduation from academy, sucked a bit of the joy and pride of achievement out of his grand weekend.

Oh well, he thought as Jessie finished her notes and stuffed the notebook back in her purse. Jessie's stories had caused a family uproar more than once. Lord knew what that plagiarized story from the movie "Summer Place" had done. He grinned at Jessie and stood up as she rose from the couch. If there'd been trouble in the parsonage, you could bet that Jessie was at the heart of it.

"Tucking notes away for the great American novel?" Enoch asked as he took Jessie's arm and headed back to the front rooms and the thinning crowd.

"I think I'll go talk to D'nardo," Jessie said. "Sounds like a decent guy. Maybe he'll see my finer side." She peeked into the bedrooms as they went down the hall. "I need the charges dropped."

Enoch waited while she spoke a few words to their parents, and then walked her out to her car.

"What are you doing?" she asked as she slipped into the driver's seat, closed the door and ran down the window. "Running interference for the alleged killer?"

"This is going to be more ugly than you think," he said as he rested his hands on the windowsill. "Without any proof that Butch abused Rachel, you may find your position untenable." He looked over the roof of her car and out at the street. "I feel like a lot of this is my fault." He watched a flock of starlings flare up into the air from a neighbor's yard and swoop out of sight over the trees that lined the street. "I always thought I was doing the right thing as I grew up but now I realize I was wrapped up in myself. I kept a lot of distance between myself and you two girls."

"We were a lot younger than you, and we were girls," Jessie said.

"But it never dawned on me that I should look out for you two, you know, be more aware of your daily lives and look to see if there were ways I could have reached out to you and been a better brother. It's like I was careful about the sins of commission, like hitting you and pulling your hair—which I never did—and I forgot about the sins of omission."

"I know," Jessie said, looking up at Enoch's earnest face and speaking in a singsong sarcastic tone. "Making sure you didn't overlook opportunities for kindness and helpfulness." She grinned at him and returned to speaking in her normal voice. "Some people go overboard with their meddling, and that makes me crazy."

"You're right," Enoch agreed, tracking the starlings where they reappeared in the distance. "I always had this sense that sticking my nose into other people's business was rude and intrusive, and unwelcome. It bedeviled me when I was a minister. I was always unsure of where to draw the line between helpfulness and prying." He looked down at Jessie. "I guess I erred on the side of avoidance. I will admit, after Rachel and Butch got married, and I had the opportunity to spend more time with them, I didn't. I honestly didn't like Butch all that much, and Rachel sort of fell into his shadow, you know, nice but not much to say." Enoch shook his head in distress.

"I wasn't overly attentive either," Jessie said. "I love Rachel as a sister, but I never felt comfortable around Butch and never looked forward to visiting."

"I wish just once that Rachel had mentioned Butch's cruelty," Enoch said. "As sad as it is to admit the truth, you know, policemen have their own code and he would have been advised to keep his hands to himself."

"I've heard about that," Jessie said, readjusting her position as she prepared to start her car.

"And you wouldn't be in this mess if I'd been more observant, perhaps, a little more nosey where it mattered."

"Don't worry about me," Jessie said as the engine came to life. "I know for a fact that prick hurt her, more than once. I know it in my bones."

"Did she ever tell you he hit her?"

"Not in those words. You know Rachel. I'm sure she believed it was her cross to bear, you know, turn the other cheek; speak kindly to those who abuse you, all that Christian crap that makes abused women believe they're not worth shit, that they deserve to be battered and beaten."

"It's not only Christian women who are battered," Enoch said.

"You're right," Jessie agreed. "There are many other brutal cultures, but Christianity wraps its doctrines up in the warm blanket of brotherly love. Then it throws in the Beatitudes, which teach meekness and humility. What it really teaches you is that you aren't worth shit from the moment you're born, that you were born in sin, and that if you don't humble yourself and grovel before the Lord, you'll never get to heaven." She released the emergency brake of her Volvo and paused.

"You're bitter," Enoch said, taking a step back from the car. "You're cynical and bitter."

"Aren't you?" Jessie asked. "What about you and Leah? What about lies and deception and people who pretend to be someone they're not? Where was Joe's wife's fidelity? Perhaps you have quite a lot in common with D'nardo."

"Well," Enoch took another step back and laughed. "At least he wasn't a minister in his former life."

Jessie blew him a flamboyant kiss as she backed up.

"You're a good brother," she called through the open window. "I'll call you tomorrow."

CHAPTER 8

The Story Behind the Story

Detective D'nardo came out to the front desk to meet Jessie. "Nice of you to stop by. How was the funeral?"

"Funereally," Jessie said.

"My shift's over," Joe said. "I honestly didn't expect you. I'm starved. Can I buy you dinner?"

"Why?" Jessie asked. "You've already got my confession."

"I just want to chat in a more pleasant setting. Don't go anywhere; I'll only be a moment." Joe stepped aside and spoke quietly with the duty officer.

"Let's walk," Joe suggested when he returned. "I've been chained to my desk all day." They exited the building and crossed the street. "Shyler doesn't boast any restaurants worth reviewing but you can depend on the veal cutlets at the Italian restaurant a block down."

The restaurant was dark and cool as they entered, like a welcoming cave in the summer woods.

"Thank god," Jessie said after a deep gulp of some nondescript Chianti. "I was about to have the DTs."

"You look barely old enough to drink."

"That's either my school girl charm," she said as she lit a second cigarette, "or an overbearing cop attitude." She blew a stream of blue gray smoke off to her left.

"Why do you smoke?" Joe asked.

"It's the overbearing cop attitude," she said.

"It's the reformed me. I quit smoking five years ago." He leaned back.

"It's the dramatic me," Jessie said. "I used to savor the old black-and-white movies where news correspondents huddled over their beat-up Underwoods wearing wide ties and rumpled dress shirts with cigarettes dangling precariously from their mouths. I wanted to be one of them." She took another drag on her cigarette. "I could never figure out why none of those guys learned to type."

Joe grinned. "Cops can't type either."

Their waiter plopped two plastic-encased menus and a large basket of fragrant bread on the table. "I'll be right back," he said.

"Too many choices," Jessie said, skimming the menu and releasing a sigh of fatigue.

"Like I said, the veal's great," Joe said. "Maybe some salad?"

"Sounds good," Jessie said as the waiter returned. Joe placed their order and handed back the menus. "What do you want?" Jessie asked.

"Are you always that direct?"

"It depends. I understand you're a direct guy, so, I assumed you like people to be direct."

"What makes you say that?"

"I do my homework, too."

"Okay," Joe conceded. "I'm stumped with this case."

"That's odd. With an alleged suspect, a dead body and a confession, you can't figure out the crime? I heard you were smart." Jessie sipped her wine and pinched a blob of warm wax running down the edge of the candle. Every table had a candle stuffed into a squat wine bottle coated with fat rings of accumulated wax. She studied the lavalike mess then raised her eyes to the large poster on the wall behind Joe's head. It was a darkened rendition of the Roman forum, rippled by moisture and preserved under a film of flyspecks and grease.

"Wait a minute," she said. "I take that back. You're not smart if you can't believe what I told you. Of all people, you should be able to see I wouldn't hit an asshole as strong as Butch if I didn't fear for my life or someone else's. You think I would walk into a fight and fill in the blanks with assumptions?" She ground her cigarette out in the ashtray with more energy than required. "My god, Rachel's life was hell! You saw her. People don't go off their rocker because of one tragic incident. Most people survive seeing violent crimes. You know that. She took one look at Butch collapsed on the floor, and it was *lights out*."

"Tell me the sequence again," Joe said.

Jessie sampled her salad. "I hate tomatoes." She picked the cherry tomatoes out of the salad and wrapped them in a napkin. "Squirties we called them when we were kids." She tucked the wrapped tomatoes under the edge of her plate. "After I hit Butch and he fell, Rachel started to pass out. I grabbed her and sat her down in a chair, pushing her head down toward her lap. I bent down and checked out Butch who was bleeding like a stuck pig. (I only wanted to stop him, not kill him.) When I looked back at Rachel, she had pulled her chair closer to the table and was resting her head on her hands. I thought she was okay."

"When did you call the police?"

"I told you all of this before. Right away."

"When did you write those notes of what happened?"

"What notes?" Jessie leaned back so the waiter could place a large platter of spaghetti and veal cutlet in front of her. She leaned forward and inhaled the rich aroma of fragrant basil-tomato sauce. Parmesan cheese was sprinkled thickly over the dish like early snow.

"I thought you didn't like tomatoes," Joe said. "The notes that were in your purse when they booked you."

"Just my habit I guess. Enoch and Officer Jackson were trying to revive Butch. I felt kind of light-headed so I anchored myself in an old habit; write what you see, what you saw."

Joe plunged his fork into his pile of thick spaghetti, wound a large mouthful and ate it. "Tell me about Butch."

Did all cops talk with their mouth full? Jessie wondered. She finished chewing her food and wiped the edges of her mouth with the checkered napkin from her lap.

"My god," she said relaxing against the back of her chair. "I didn't realize how hungry a loved one's funeral could make me." She gave Joe a shameful grin. "Sorry. I really hated that son-of-a-bitch."

"I heard he'd had a tough life," Joe said. "Alcoholic father, mother beaten to death by his father in a drunken rage, tour of duty in 'Nam. Hasn't held any job long enough to get ahead." Joe looked up from his plate. "His father come to the funeral?"

"No. He didn't even attend their wedding. He would have had to sober up. You know those C.R.O.W.s. No drinking allowed."

"Crows?"

"Circle of Redemption of the World," Jessie said. "The religion of my family; I'm an outcast." She pointed cryptically at the wine, the snuffed cigarette and her earrings. "Very bad."

"I understand Butch Vogel's real name was Merriam Webster Vogel. Strange name for a guy of his description and background."

"Claims his mother was a real educated woman, or wanted to be." Jessie broke off another piece of bread and slathered it with soft yellow butter. "I don't think she ever finished college. Butch said that was one of the things that attracted him to Rachel, that she was educated."

"Tell me about her."

"She's my sister," Jessie said. "Journalism 101 says you cannot be objective about your own family or friends."

"Cheat," Joe said with a laugh. "Truth is, we need her. She's our only witness."

"She was born six years before me, back when our family lived in Cleveland, Ohio. My father was assistant minister there. She was blond and beautiful in all her baby pictures. Actually right up until she was about five and got that thyroid disease that made her eyes bulge out of their sockets. I don't remember her very much until I was maybe fourish which would make her about ten. My parents stopped taking pictures of her after she got sick."

"I'm not a medical expert but thyroid disease usually isn't the end of the world," Joe said as he sipped his wine and filled his mouth with food. "She doesn't look so bad."

"As she grew older, and with medication, her eyes receded somewhat and of course, her skull grew bigger, so no, now, she doesn't look so bad. But she was never much to look at with her big eyes and the coke bottle bottoms she wore for glasses. In school all the kids called her four-eyes and other nasty names. The epithet that stuck and hurt the most was Popeye. She hated that."

"I understand she's an office manager for a legal firm in Madison. Worked there since she got married."

"She's a steady Eddie. Good Christian: reliable, honest, diligent, dependable. She's the main breadwinner in the family."

"What's the story on Butch? I'm told he couldn't hold a job."

"Butch had delusions of grandeur. He'd take a job as a used car salesman and tell everyone he was the general manager. Went to work in a sheet metal plant and told everyone he was a design engineer. Took a job on a construction site and told everyone he was the site supervisor. I don't remember the details but he always got fired. Claimed everyone had it in for him. Said he was getting backlash for serving his country in Vietnam. Said nobody respected a soldier." Jessie stopped to eat for a few moments. "Said the world was against him. Frankly," she looked Joe in the eye, "I think he took all his failures and frustrations out on Rachel." She paused then and sat in serious thought for a moment. "You know? I have seen him be nasty to Rachel a few times, but come to think of it, in public, he was the poster child for 'Mister Nice Guy'." She shook her head. "But I know different. I know that something happened last Sunday afternoon. I just don't know what. Everything I've ever feared or believed was wrong with that marriage was in Rachel's voice when she called me last Sunday. I know it."

"You said you didn't speak with her." Joe watched her keenly as though he could detect inconsistencies if he observed her carefully enough.

"It was the tone of her voice on my answering machine. I'd never heard her sound like that, I don't know, strained, stressed, something. Not fear exactly, more like expired fear, past fear."

"Did you call her back? Try to find out what was wrong?"

"I tried. The phone was busy."

"I heard you didn't come around that much," Joe said. "Didn't spend a lot of time at Rachel's house, didn't cotton much to the old family homestead. Was it Rachel's tone of voice that made you come out Sunday evening?"

"Yes. Yes. And no. I don't cotton much to the family homestead as you so colorfully put it. My parents bought their present house a year after I'd put some miles between their lives and mine, after Dad retired from the ministry. I don't think I've slept in that house three times in the past six years. It doesn't feel like any home of mine and frankly, I didn't like any of the others much either." Jessie inverted the tines of her fork and tapped them on the edge of her plate. "As for Rachel, I tried to visit when I could, mostly came for dinner. Sometimes we played Scrabble after we did the dishes. Butch would start the game with us then walk away to watch TV. Rude bastard."

Jessie attacked her diminishing plate of food with renewed gusto. "This is really good. I could live on pasta."

"And your reason for driving out last Sunday without calling Rachel back? She didn't say anything specific? You heard a cry for help, and that's it?"

"Is that so strange?" Jessie asked, her cheeks flushing with irritation.

"Sorry," Joe said, holding up his left hand in mock resistance. "I didn't mean to upset you. But Enoch did tell me it wasn't like you to come running to help the family. Said you weren't too comfortable with the religion and the restraints in your home. Said you always chaffed under the strict demands of your church."

"C.R.O.W.s. Not my church." Jessie sat back to let her temper cool a bit then leaned closer to her plate and said, "Enoch is right. I didn't stick around much, and frankly, I was so glad to move out of home in my freshman year at college that I didn't let the door bang me on my ass." She chewed another mouthful of food and reflected. "You can't imagine what it was like growing up in that house; self-righteous preacher running our lives, dictating how we should think, and treating my mother like a cipher. He was all smiles and radiance standing behind his pulpit and preaching to his flock on Sabbath mornings.

"Always warning us about sin, sex, slothfulness and such, while he charmed the ladies like the Pied Piper. At home he was cold and unsympathetic, quick to accuse and swift to punish. In public he was outgoing, friendly, caring, and comforting." She grinned at Joe. "Like the Good Shepherd without the long hair and robes." She sipped her wine. "Actually more like a wolf in sheep's clothing." A slight expression of discovery came over her face. "Though I could never see what Rachel saw in Butch, maybe, just maybe, she subconsciously found a mate like her father. I've heard that's not uncommon."

Her look reflected frustration with herself. "I'll admit: It took me a long time to see the real man, my father, though since I was little, I have watched people very carefully."

"I'll bet you have." Joe smiled and continued eating.

"Oh shit!" Jessie exclaimed. "Why am I telling you all of this? You'd think you were the reporter and I the interviewee." She cocked her head to one side and said, "What I should simply say is that Rachel married a person a lot like Father, Mr. Nice Guy for the world to see, but at home and in his heart, the Devil incarnate."

"Can you prove that?" Joe asked. "About your brother-in-law, I mean?" He emptied his wine glass and refilled both glasses from the bottle on the table. "What does your attorney say? Who'd you hire?"

"Certainly not that frumpy nerd you saw at the arraignment. Took me a while to get connected but I'm meeting with Ben Levine, Boston's finest." Jessie put her fork down and leaned back against her chair. "I'm stuffed." She smiled and wiped her mouth with her napkin. "If you didn't have my confession, you know, I wouldn't give you spit."

"I know."

***

To say the large city newsroom went silent when Jessie walked in a week after the murder would be a gross exaggeration. Newsrooms are never silent until the last reporter has left and the last police scanner has been unplugged, which never happened, not at the Boston Beacon.

Heads lifted, eyes stared and chatter dropped off as Jessie came through the large double doors on Monday, July 19th. The suffocating blast of stale cigarette smoke hit her, lending a sense of the familiar, like coming home. As she strode past the rows of cluttered desks, a reporter called, "Hello," and said, "Your phone's been ringing off the hook for the last five minutes. Your pager off?"

Jessie ignored the question, shoved a toppled pile of folders aside to uncover her ringing phone and dropped into her battered chair, grabbing a pencil and note pad in the process.

"They what?" she cried. She slammed the pencil down, snapping it in half. "That's ridiculous! Meeting where? When? I'll be right there. You tell those sons-of-bitches to wait until I get there. Right."

Without another word, Jessie flew around the rows of desks in the fluorescent gray room, waved hello and good-bye to her editor in his corner office with smoked glass walls, and burst through the double doors, leaving a room of people behind her staring and curious. She laughed to herself as she ran down the broad granite steps of the elegant 19th century newspaper

UNWORTHY

building and raced across the street dodging between cars to reach the parking lot.

You think cops are nosy? She mused to herself picturing the room of people she'd left behind. Reporters are relentless. Try hiding something from a reporter, a good one, like me. She waved to the attendant in the tiny shack by the entrance to the parking lot and ran to her car. Inside she threw her ubiquitous bulging purse on the front seat and screeched her car backwards out of her parking slot. Get out of the way, you poky bastard, she mouthed to the old man ambling along the sidewalk where she needed to exit. I can outfox a cop any day. Don't I know how to dig out that telltale detail that moves a common crime story from page three to page one? I'll tell you about nosy.

She sat at the red light, impatiently tapping her left foot on the floor. Stringer, she recalled, thinking back to her first days of glory. Just a stringer, a little college girl who begged and wheedled for any scrap the newspaper would toss her. Any chance they would give her to write a story, follow a lead, show those big city editors that she was a good reporter.

The light changed and Jessie pushed the gas pedal to the floor, laying two small strips of rubber on the city street. She took a sharp left and then a right and another left, shooting out onto Storrow Drive between two speeding trucks. The meeting in Danvers was in twenty minutes. They'd better wait for her, or else.

In a desperate effort to avoid thinking about the meeting ahead, she let her mind wander back to her day in the sun in 1972, barely four years ago. She'd done it! She'd poked around late at a political party while most of the people were drifting away. The speeches were over; the booze was drunk; and banners were collapsing. The other reporters had departed to write their stories. But she had decided to take one more tour around the restrooms and backstage. There she'd found it. Gold! The main speaker of the evening, a pontifical senator from the tony section on the North

Shore was fucking a black woman, who later was identified as his chief opponent.

She smiled broadly as she sped through traffic and raced up the ramp to 93 North. That was a story. True, it was the story behind the story, but that was headlines, big time, above the fold! God, how the fireworks had exploded! That was the end for Miss In-Your-Face Black, Beautiful and Bleeding Heart, sponsor for the underdog. All the defiance and victimization claiming in the world couldn't get her a job as dogcatcher. Of course, the senator was reelected that fall in a landslide. Was that fair? Not by a damned sight. It was reality. It was still a man's world.

She laughed, glanced in her rear view mirror and switched lanes. She had her beefs with feminism, but it did have its points. However, most of the feminists she knew had burned their bras and found significant others among their own sex. How was that going to win their battles?

Jessie cut sharply across two lanes of traffic to make the Danvers exit. If I don't get behind a dump truck or a school bus, I'll make it on time, she thought.

CHAPTER 9

Castle on the Hill

As Jessie turned in through the curved brick entry to Danvers State Mental Hospital, she studied the filigree wrought iron gates that stood open and welcoming, though the tall wrought iron fence that spread out as far as she could see on either side clearly stated that leaving was quite a different matter.

She followed the blacktop driveway up Hathorne Hill, coming to a stop in a small parking lot in front of an imposing castle-like building right out of a Gothic novel. For a moment she stood beside her car to study the imposing brick facade pierced by fortress-like towers that rose into the blue sky above, a dark contrast to the bright July morning. Between two sharp-peaked gables the central tower rose through six floors, giving great emphasis to the main entrance below. She shuddered as she started up the stone steps flanked by low granite abutments. Her normally cheery outlook gave way to a sense of awe and horror that she should be entering this institution made infamous in the fifties by stories of shock therapy and lobotomies, overcrowding and neglectful treatment, an open sore in the state's mental health program, still controversial and spurned.

Inside the arched entry, her awe turned to an overwhelming sense of gloom and depression. Did anyone who entered this door ever exit alive? Was there only one way out of this building, a tiny numbered grave on the grassy slopes that separated this medieval institution from the world of sanity and freedom below? She stopped at the high counter that served as the visitors' desk and found it difficult to state her sister's name in what felt more to her like a house of horrors than an institution for the mentally insane.

Mutely, Jessie followed a slovenly old woman in a dull blue uniform down a wide hall along the front of the building to a large room in the east wing. Clustered near a tall window covered with a gauzelike ragged shade, she found her family, Detective D'nardo and three strangers.

"What the hell is going on here?" Jessie said in a low voice as she hurried forward to hug her sister who drooped in a canvas wheelchair next to a white-coated orderly. Jessie's voice, though hushed in tone, produced a weak echo in the cavernous room, bare except for some folding chairs lined up along the walls. Near an empty cement fireplace she saw pictures of fireworks tacked on a bulletin board bearing punctures from millions of tacks. The resulting wounds in the cork made her wonder that it could support a square of toilet paper. Scotch-taped above the pictures, in fat orange letters, were the words, *Happy Fourth of July*.

Leaving her unresponsive sister, Jessie took a chair opposite the Holy Three, as her remaining family members had formed themselves in her mind since last week in the hospital waiting room. She looked at Enoch; he probably was a saint. She couldn't think of one unkind or cruel thing he had ever done in his life.

She quietly studied her father, his rigidly erect shoulders and pious expression. Her father was a mystery, appearing lofty and godlike while Jessie picked up on vibes that linked him more with the underworld than heaven. She had not one shred of evidence to support her belief in his nefarious Bible toting persona, though as an adult she'd come to understand his insistence that his children kiss the hand that punished them was pretty twisted. Amorphous things fluttered in the quiet chambers of her memory, like cringing at her father's touch, and her mother's quiet crying in the night. But she had nothing substantive. So Jessie had never confronted her father. She'd settled for silently withholding her trust.

And next to God's chosen one sat her mother Willa. Willa was plain, simple, and pathetic. For years she'd been a fraud in public where she'd performed the role of a preacher's wife like a robot, yet had been a contradiction at home. Grown up and living on her own, Jessie could now see how Willa had vacillated between competent housewife and mother and frightened wraith teetering on the edge of insanity. (Well, Jessie reminded herself, that's a little dramatic.) Sad and depressed might be more realistic. Long ago Jessie had determined that turning to her mother for emotional support was like leaning on a strand of boiled spaghetti.

Not a word had been uttered since Jessie's arrival. The silence of this ghoulish gathering made her nervous. Jessie looked around at the others and asked, "Is this a meeting to help Rachel, or have I traveled back in time to the Spanish Inquisition?"

Floyd cleared his throat, positioned his Bible on his right knee, and began speaking. "We are gathered together—Oh god, Jessie thought irreverently, don't tell me he is going to preach a sermon—to address a grave situation, specifically, Rachel's state of mind, and in addition, charges from her employer of misconduct."

"We are talking felony here," the attorney representing the legal firm where Rachel had worked for six years said, "not misconduct."

"I know I'm not acting in the role of a reporter here," Jessie said, sitting on the edge of her metal chair and looking directly at each person in the small circle, "but wouldn't it be better to give our names and state our interests here, for the record, or off the record, I should say." Her courageous stab at structure ended in a self-conscious mumble. The question, *What in the hell are we all doing here?* ran screaming through her head. Perhaps this is what they call an out-of-body experience. She felt for the reassurance of substance by gripping her fat purse in her lap and looked around the forbidding room for little green men in the shadows.

"I think everyone knows I'm Floyd Keller, father of Rachel Vogel, and this is Willa Keller, Rachel's mother. Next to her is Enoch, our son, who serves on the Shyler Police force." Floyd gestured toward Joe to continue.

"I'm Detective Joseph D'nardo of the Shyler Police Department, here to gain insight into Rachel's condition and hopefully an assessment of her recovery potential. My investigation of the death of Merriam Webster Vogel, better known as Butch Vogel, requires we exert ourselves fully to gain Rachel's presence in pretrial testimony as a key witness to her husband's death." He glanced aside at the man to his left.

"I'm Attorney Christopher Gallagher, outside legal advisor to the firm of Penn, Foster and Gabler, where Rachel Vogel was employed until the death of her husband on July 12, 1976. In the week of her absence, her employer has uncovered what we believe to be a serious case of defalcation, embezzlement from trust funds. My job is to perform initial investigations into the status of her mental health for purposes of proceeding against her with criminal charges."

Only Jessie gasped in disbelief. It was obvious the others had already been informed of Rachel's crime, thus the alarm in her brother's voice on the phone earlier that morning. She took a deep breath to compose herself.

"I'm Jessie Keller, Rachel's sister."

D'nardo cast a cryptic look at Jessie then returned to scribbling on his note pad.

Willa sniffled.

Finally the young man in a white lab coat spoke. "I'm Austin Croteau, a licensed clinical social worker, employed by the Commonwealth of Massachusetts at this facility. Upon Rachel Vogel's admission, I was assigned to manage her case. The gentleman sitting next to Rachel is Ted Birkensaw, an orderly. I believe each of you has your own agenda regarding my patient, Mrs. Vogel." Austin stopped to open a three-ringed binder and select a tabbed section. "My understanding is that Mrs. Vogel's presence during the alleged murder of her husband led to her present condition and that she is wanted as a witness in that case, and further, she is charged with embezzlement by her employer and is wanted for questioning on that charge."

Austin finished his recital and looked around the room, his expression flat as though his pronouncements were final. He pushed his dark-rimmed glasses back up on his nose.

God, what an arrogant little man, Jessie thought. I think he's acting above his authority.

"That's all painfully obvious," Jessie said. "What those of us who have an agenda, as you so delicately phrased it, and those of us who don't, really need, is a statement from a psychiatric doctor regarding Rachel's diagnosis and prognosis for recovery. Are you prepared to issue that?"

Austin peered at Jessie with a frown of irritation bordering on hostility, his eyes narrowing behind his thick lenses. He glanced furtively around the circle, letting his eyes rest for a moment on Rachel's limp and bedraggled form. He shuffled his feet, sat a little straighter, and flipped to another tabbed section of his binder. Looking up and then back at the typed page in front of him, he pushed his glasses back on his nose and read, "Mrs. Rachel Vogel, resident of Shyler, Massachusetts, was committed to the Danvers State Mental Hospital for a period of ten days for a full examination regarding her mental and emotional condition."

As Croteau's monotone voice droned on, Jessie's mind wandered off to the taciturn detective, Sergeant Friday, in the old TV series, *Dragnet*. She sat on her hands to control the urge to stand up and scream at the blithering idiot in the scuffed brown shoes and heinous tie, "Shut the fuck up and give us the facts, man, just the facts!"

"So my assessment concludes with the diagnosis of schizophrenia, subject to be treated with medication as prescribed by a supervisory psychiatrist. We cannot predict her recovery, but we believe the potential is low. We do not anticipate Mrs. Vogel will be able to play a constructive role as a witness in a criminal case, nor face charges in a legal case."

"Is this your opinion or the opinion of a qualified psychiatrist?" Floyd asked. Austin looked up from his binder and pushed his glasses up on his nose with his right index finger, wrinkling his upper lip in the process.

"I have completed my assessment and reports for my supervisor who is out of town this week at a conference. Upon his return next Monday, he will read my assessment and affix his approval."

"How do you know he will agree with your assessment?" Joe asked. "Has he seen Rachel? Has he diagnosed her?"

"Detective D'nardo," Austin Croteau said firmly, "you were given permission to sit in on this meeting but were informed you did not have standing in these communications or decisions." He glared at D'nardo and added, "I am correct in that, am I not?"

"Correct."

"Then if we are all agreed on this disposition for Mrs. Vogel," Austin said, looking around the circle with an air of expectancy and making a note on a sheet of paper, "I'll go over this case with my supervisor and we will petition the court for commitment for a period that he recommends."

"What's he saying?" Willa whispered loudly into Floyd's ear. "I don't understand."

"Rachel is being committed," Floyd said.

"No!" Willa screamed, jumping to her feet and running over and grasping Rachel's shoulders from behind. "You can't do that to her! You can't keep her here! She's coming home with us." Dropping her voice to a low croon, Willa bent over her daughter's rumpled hair and pulled the tangled strands back over her shoulders saying, "I'll take care of you Rachel, just like I took care of you when you were little. I'll comb your hair out nice and maybe we could put it into braids. Would you like that?"

"Willa!" Floyd said in a commanding tone. "Sit down!"

Enoch and Jessie exchanged shocked glances at hearing their father's *at home* voice in public. Enoch rose to take control of his mother and Jessie looked over at Joe. In controlled but grim tones she asked, "Is this what you wanted to observe?" She turned to the attorney who sat smoking a cigar and tapping his ash on the floor. "You still want to press charges?"

***

"You just came from where?" Attorney Benjamin Levine slammed his open palm on his huge rosewood and chrome desk and thrust his potbelly forward against the edge.

"You went to a meeting with your sister, a detective, a lawyer, and…the whole frigging world? I told you to stay to yourself and keep your mouth shut!" He calmed down a level, tossed his pewter-rimmed glasses on the bare desk and said, "Or would you like to represent yourself? Perhaps you know more than I do. Perhaps you have passed the Massachusetts bar and have defended numerous high profile cases. Perhaps," he added, letting out a huge sigh of frustration, "perhaps you should take over writing case law, maybe revise the Commonwealth of Massachusetts Criminal Practice procedures."

Though Jessie was scared by few and cowed by no one, she shrank an inch lower in the maroon leather chair that already dwarfed her small frame. She waited until the rage in the air thinned and said, "I'm sorry, Mr. Levine. I was only acting in the interest of my sister. She's so helpless."

"I'm helpless!" Ben said in exasperation. "I'm the one who is trying to get charges dropped with a dead brother-in-law, a well-fingerprinted copper pot and an insane witness. I'm helpless if you keep playing wild and free with your life instead of following my advice." He paused and stared at her, his glance warning of his forthcoming comment. "I'd have thought my hourly rate would have precluded your wish to flaunt your independence." Again, letting out a deep breath, and running his short stubby fingers through his thinning red hair, he resettled himself comfortably in the high-backed leather chair that also dwarfed his short, squat body. Sounding more like a frustrated but caring father than an enraged attorney, he said, "I know you consider yourself to be a bright and accomplished reporter. I know you are quick with a phrase and keen to get the scoop, but, and I'm only going to say this to you one more time." His voice returned to that of an enraged lawyer. "You are not a lawyer! You do not know the law! If you infect my efforts with your own foolishness and stupidity, I will withdraw from representing you!"

Ben Levine swung around in his chair and stared out the wall of glass that overlooked the Charles River and more specifically, the complex roof of the central octagonal section of the Charles Street Jail. The four wings of Quincy granite spread out from the center, reminding Ben, once again, of how many of the state's historic institutions needed to be closed and perhaps recycled to more civilized purposes. With a smart kick of his wing tipped shoe, he shot his chair around and faced Jessie again.

"Let's get to work." He pressed a button on the console on his desk and requested the State vs. Keller case file. When his secretary had closed the door behind her, he began. "Your defense depends on the ability to prove that you knew of past physical abuse by Mr. Vogel and that when you entered the kitchen and found them fighting, you acted in reaction to that knowledge."

"What do you mean, my defense?" Jessie asked, sitting straighter. "I thought you were going to get the charges dropped."

"While I work to that end, we must lose no time in filing motions and requests, and proceeding as though the case will be tried. So far, my phone calls to the District Attorney have met with blind resistance. So, give me the facts. How many times did Butch physically harm Rachel? When? Where? How do you come by these facts?"

CHAPTER 10

Back to the Scene of the Crime

At the Shyler Police station, D'nardo waited near Enoch's locker for Officer Keller to sign in. "You've got to be the only cop I know who leaves his weapon at work," Joe said as Enoch completed getting into uniform.

Enoch acknowledged Joe's comment and explained his circumstances as he buckled on the heavy belt. "When I graduated from the police academy, I didn't have the energy to set up housekeeping alone, so I moved in with my parents. Mom was glad to have me home again, but I could see that Father was having a hard time with my new career. So, rather than make them both uncomfortable, I abided by their request to store my gun and other unsightly police paraphernalia at the station." He pinned his silver badge to the freshly laundered and pressed uniform shirt and closed his locker door.

"Got authorization to take you off street duty this afternoon," Joe said.

"Why?" Enoch snapped the padlock through the holes in the locker handle.

"I'm having a difficult time putting together the facts for Butch Vogel's alleged murder and I was hoping you could help me. We'll take my car."

When Joe and Enoch arrived at Rachel Vogel's house they found Old Charlie sitting in his '65 Tempest reading the Boston Beacon and sipping a cold cup of coffee.

"Who's that?" Joe asked as he pulled over to the curb and cut the engine.

"Sullivan," Enoch said. "They call him Old Charlie. Been on the force forever. Suffers from arthritis. Takes all the observation jobs he can get that allow him to sit down. Good guy."

Joe slapped the fender of Old Charlie's car as he and Enoch approached from the back. Old Charlie jumped. When he saw Enoch's uniform he tucked his newspaper down beside the door. Joe flashed his ID. "Hi fellas," Old Charlie said. "What's doin'?"

"Going in to do a little investigation," Joe said. "See much of the family upstairs?"

"The mother goes to work every day. Takes the little girl and the baby and drops them off at her mother's house. Comes home after five. Stays put most evenings."

"See anyone else coming or going?" Joe asked.

"Her brother comes once in a while, late evening. Stays a couple of hours then leaves."

"Thanks, Charlie," Enoch said as he and Joe walked around the car and ducked under the black and yellow crime scene tape. They went up the steps to the front porch.

"Woman doesn't have a brother," Joe mumbled as he turned the key in the lock. Enoch looked at Joe and entered the front hall, leading the way through the dining room and into the kitchen.

Shut up in the July heat and humidity, the house had a stale odor, like a room of unwashed sheets and damp bath towels. Butch's blood had begun to dry and crack on the embossed linoleum surface. The window shades had been drawn by the police to discourage peepers. Joe went over and raised the shade over the kitchen sink. Enoch switched on the ceiling light and waited for instructions from Joe.

"Okay," Joe said, moving back to stand just beyond the archway between the kitchen and the dining room. He motioned for Enoch to move farther into the dining room. "Jessie met you at the front door. You and Officer Jackson came through the front hall, through the dining room and into the kitchen. Tell me everything that caught your eye on that route."

Enoch set his feet apart and grasped his hands behind himself to think, looking like a soldier at parade rest. "There's nothing in the hall, as you saw, and except for the dining room table, six chairs and a small buffet, nothing in the dining room. Oh, wait a minute." Enoch walked back toward the front hall and stared at the vacuum cleaner now pushed against the dining room wall. "I think the vacuum cleaner was more in the middle of the floor. We tripped over it." Enoch looked around and moved toward the kitchen. "Other than that, Jessie was clinging to me; Rachel was sitting motionless at the table; and Butch was lying on the floor. The pots and pans were strewn about pretty much as you see them now."

"The vacuum cleaner probably got smashed against the wall when the EMTs tried to get by with the stretcher," Joe said. Moving into the kitchen behind Enoch, he pointed to the baker's rack. "Jessie admits to putting that back upright and pushing it against the wall."

"I know it's none of my business," Enoch said, "but, what is it you're struggling with? I normally don't mind a crime scene, but this one is too personal."

"Let's go into the living room," Joe suggested. He took a seat in an overstuffed chair, probably Early Depression, circa 1930s, Joe thought. Enoch sat tentatively on the mustard-colored couch, hovering on the edge of a lumpy cushion. "Somebody here like to read?" Joe asked, noting three bookshelves packed with books.

"Rachel," Enoch said. "Butch wasn't much for reading. Even when I knew him in the army, he'd sneak out to a card game rather than pick up a book, though as assistant to the chaplain, he wasn't supposed to gamble."

"You knew Butch in the army?" Joe asked with surprise. "How is it I don't know that?"

"I guess you never asked."

"Look," Joe said, leaning back into the threadbare chair and making himself comfortable. "I want to know every fucking detail you know about Merriam Webster Vogel. I want to know what he ate for breakfast, when he took a shit and if he wiped himself when he was done."

"I've never attempted to hold back anything," Enoch said, showing his affront at Joe's crude language by his diffident response. "Truth be told, all I've been able to think about is Rachel, Jessie, and my poor mother."

"Sorry for the crap," Joe said, raising his hands, palms out, to indicate he was done with the attack. "I've investigated many cases in my day and helped put a lot of perps behind bars, but something about this whole thing is wrong, wrong, wrong. I let my irritation out on you. Sorry."

"Butch wasn't exactly an open book," Enoch began. He eased himself back to lean against the couch cushions but never relaxed into a comfortable position. "Quite the opposite, in fact." He rested one foot on a knee, then switched. The toe of his shiny black uniform shoe came within inches of Butch's family Bible. "There's an example." Enoch pointed to the Bible with his shoe. "A few years ago Butch came home with that book and told Rachel it was his mother's family Bible, the only thing she'd left him. I thought it odd at the time because he'd lost track of his father after he'd joined the army and said his mother had been killed before that."

"What's inside?" Joe asked, leaning forward but not leaving his chair.

"Damned if I know. It's locked and Rachel told me he never let her look at it."

"Okay," Joe said, leaning back again. "Tell me about something about which you know something. What was he like in the army? How long did you know him? How'd he meet Rachel?" Joe looked keenly at Enoch. "Sorry I'm so slow getting to know all you guys.

Were you the chaplain Butch assisted? Where did you serve? What happened?"

As the hot July sun moved past its zenith and started its slow descent to the West, Enoch told Joe parts of his own story, weaving in facts about Butch, what little he knew.

"So Butch meets Rachel when he comes home with you Christmas '65 and marries her two weeks later? Sounds like a throwback to the '40s when marriages happened on the docks as guys were shipping out. Why the rush?"

"You'd have to know Rachel and understand our upbringing. Plus, Rachel never tells much. Always kept most things to herself when we were kids. Probably stemmed from the problem with her eyes and feeling she was ugly. My guess is, Butch pushed her for sex and she married him to avoid the sin of fornication."

"The sin of fornication?" Joe asked with a chuckle. "That your preacher talk coming out?"

"Not many guys want to let a woman hold them off. Certainly not today with women initiating sex half the time. Sometimes I wish I'd sampled the merchandise and put it back on the shelf." Enoch's voice trailed off as he looked away from Joe and feigned reading the cover of the National Geographic on the coffee table next to Butch's Bible.

"Is that what made you change your profession?" Joe asked. "I'm not trying to pry. Don't answer that if you don't want to."

"Actually, I don't mind now as much as I did," Enoch said. He dropped his foot to the floor. "I thought I'd been called to minister to God's flock, but serving as a police officer has turned out to be a better fit for me. At least I deal with people at a more honest level than the facade everyone puts up in church, lay people and clergy alike. In uniform, a cop's a cop and people expect us to see them at their worst. While I served as a chaplain in the military, it was obvious the guys cleaned up their speech and habits when I was around. Even when I was assistant pastor and serving the youth groups here in the US, I sensed nothing was truly genuine."

He looked at Joe, his expression open and questioning. "You were raised Catholic? Right?" Joe nodded. "Why is it we all put on a false face of piety when we encounter things of God, like God can't see our every move and read our every thought?"

Joe nodded his head in agreement and dropped his small notebook on his lap.

Enoch continued. "If I'd been a little less focused on things of heaven and more understanding of things on earth, I might have realized that leaving Leah alone while I finished my stint in the service would not be the smart thing to do."

"What happened?" Joe asked. "The ol' Dear John letter?"

"That would have been kind. No, Leah never wrote me anything but sweet, loving letters telling me how much she loved me, missed me and couldn't wait for me to come home. I treasured every letter, reading them over and over at night and picturing the rest of our life together, me serving in the ministry, she making a home for our children and me, growing closer and closer over the years, growing gray together." Enoch stopped and sat forward laughing at himself. "Trust me, Joe. Silly teenage girls with fantasies of knights in shining armor have nothing on a love-besotted naive young man who has saved himself for that perfect woman with whom he will share his life and heart." Enoch laughed again and sat back.

"We were married for six years and couldn't have any children. Oh, by the way, that reminds me. As I said, I didn't know much about Butch and Rachel's private life, though she did tell me once that Butch was angry she hadn't conceived. She said she'd tried and tried—I thought she was going to stop there—but she went on to say that Butch was so experienced, and expected her to do things she didn't want to do. She also said he blamed her for their lack of children because he knew for a fact he was fertile, had a few slant-eyed brats running around 'Nam to prove it."

"Nice guy." Joe snorted with disgust.

"Anyway, Leah and I went to be checked out to see where the

problem of infertility lay and what remedies we could use. Leah was still in the examination room where the doctor had done an in-depth examination of her internal organs after his preliminary exam had raised some questions the week before. While Leah was getting dressed, the doctor motioned for me to come into his private office. He closed the door and sat down behind his large desk piled high with medical journals and books. He was an avid researcher and kept up with the newest innovations in his field. He leaned back in his chair, took a deep breath, then came forward and flattened both long-fingered hands on the glass covering his desk. I can still see his aging, ridged fingernails.

"'Your wife will never bear you a child.' He looked me in the eye. 'Not you or any other man.' I must have dropped my jaw in shock because he offered me a glass of water. 'Your wife's female organs have been carved up like cheap hamburger in the worst abortion job I've ever seen.' He just sat there, his shoulders hunched forward and his white lab coat standing away from his skinny neck. 'I trust you know nothing of this.' He nodded and said, 'I didn't think so.' After a few minutes to allow me to compose myself he said, 'I'll tell your wife the results privately and let you two work out the rest. Your only option now is adoption. I wish you luck.' About that time, Leah entered the doctor's office and I left them alone. I went out in the waiting room and left a message with the nurse for Leah that I'd be waiting in the car."

Joe looked steadily into Enoch's eyes. "I'm sure you've heard my story. Sounds like we both could have used better judgment in the wife department."

Joe tapped his fingers on his notebook and studied the narrow bars of light surrounding the drawn window shades behind the sheer curtains. The room was encased in late afternoon shadows giving the ceramic birds on the bookcase an appearance of flying into dusk. Joe studied the birds and let his memories of his grandmother drift through his mind.

"My grandmother used to say the sweet singing blackbirds held the souls of those in purgatory until the judgment day. Do you think that's possible?"

"Our religion doesn't believe in purgatory," Enoch said. "As for birds, we did study ancient religions and cultures. We learned about augury, the art of divination by observing the behavior of birds. It was practiced by the Etrurians and the Romans, some more focused on the study of entrails than patterns of flight."

"I'm about ready to resort to necromancy," Joe said. "I'm sure Butch knows who killed him." He smiled at his own absurdity. "You believe Jessie's story?"

Enoch brought his dulled gaze sharply to Joe's face, surprise and concern shading the questions he asked. "Jessie's story? You mean her memory of the incident? You think she's leaving something out or not telling the truth?"

Joe studied Enoch's face and said in a steady tone, "I mean her whole story, from beginning to end. I don't believe a word of it, well, except for Rachel's phone call. I think she's protecting Rachel though I can't figure out why."

Enoch leaned forward as though seeking enlightenment in Joe's expression. "Are you saying that Jessie's lying? That she didn't kill Butch? That Rachel did?" He shook his head in small jerks unable to accept this possibility. "Jessie never lies. All Jessie's life she wrote stories. She wrote about people in the neighborhood. She wrote about her friends at school. Sometimes she wrote fantastic tales from her imagination. But Jessie knows truth from fiction. She's a reporter; she stays focused on the facts. She may bend the rules a bit to get the story—I think all reporters do. She may manipulate her sources to get to the bottom of things, but Jessie doesn't lie. She's too professional for that."

"Would you trust her gut instincts?"

"I think I would, Joe."

"Well, I'd very much like to but instincts don't stand up in court." Joe flipped his notebook closed and slapped it face down on his leg. "My thoughts run in endless loops, questions that repeat themselves, over and over. What if Jessie owes Rachel a great debt? What if Jessie is motivated by guilt for something from the past? What if Jessie wants to protect Rachel? What if she believes Rachel would be unable to survive the rigors of an investigation, a trial, revealing the truth about her marriage, perhaps incarceration? Believe you me, I can't find any proof that Butch abused Rachel, but it's always a possibility." Joe stood up and looked about the room like he could find substantive evidence for his assumptions. "You haven't been a cop long enough to see the things I've seen. I've met some slippery eels. There are men who know how to beat a woman and not leave a mark. There are ways to bust up a person's guts without leaving a bruise." He motioned for Enoch to precede him to the front hall as he finished his thoughts. "I know there are ways to abuse a person that only require movement of the lips; words that cut and lacerate and belittle and browbeat; words that carve deep gouges in the heart and mind. I've seen the results of that too."

Chapter 11

Stormy Waters

Rachel squinted and tilted her head to the right. The buxom woman facing her tipped to the left at a sharp angle, like a ship riding up the side of an ocean swell. Rachel held the blue clad protruding breasts and stomach at this dangerous angle for a few moments then tilted her head to the left and let the behemoth with the tiny pinpoints for eyes try to right herself, in vain.

Until this strange person, with the eclipsed-moon face, removed herself from in front of Rachel and ceased pressing her with crazy questions, Rachel had decided the best solution was to make her sea sick. Right, left, the rudderless vessel before her rocked to Rachel's will. For once, Rachel was in control; her will be done.

Husbands! The woman was asking. Who knew anything about husbands? The smoky moon face insisted on asking again. It was none of her business. I'll close my eyes. I'll run away. I won't be here.

Rachel was sitting in church between her older brother Enoch and younger sister Jessie, helping her mother keep an eye on Jessie in case she misbehaved. Jessie always squirmed. Rachel was too little to have a husband; that was for mothers. See? There was Daddy now, standing straight and tall behind the pulpit, asking the congregation to follow him as he turned to a chapter in the Bible and continued talking about…his words drifted away. The early spring sunlight poured through the colored glass windows of the church scattering prisms of light over his handsome face, his spotless white shirt and his dark gray Sabbath suit.

Something dark gray pushed up from inside Rachel, but she pushed back, hard. Up front was the daddy she liked to think about, not that old daddy who used to frighten her when he swung her up on his shoulders and carried her out toward the meadows to watch the birds. That old daddy would swing her around to face him and nuzzle her tummy. Then he'd nip at her chubby legs and kiss her peepee, his tongue warm and wet. That daddy, with his face between her legs, was just a shadow now, barely a memory. This daddy whose face danced in the rainbow of glass colors, was sharp and clear. He never came near her any more, and she knew why he didn't; she was ugly.

Rachel stole a glance at her mother's face, reassuring herself of her mother's loving expression, always demonstrating her attentiveness to every word Daddy spoke. This was the example her mother set for her children and for all the church members. This was her mother's Sabbath face, worn every Sabbath since Rachel could remember. It brought comfort to Rachel and a sense of well-being that had to last her for a whole week.

Rachel closed her eyes more tightly, holding the vision of church inside her eyelids, fondling her memory gently, like stroking a cuddly kitten. She knew when she opened her eyes the vision would be gone. She held her breath and hoped the big breasts with the straining buttons would disappear into the prisms of light that were melting into the arched ceiling rafters above her daddy's head.

"Rachel," the fat black lips continued in their rich, throaty voice. "I know you're in there. That's the first time you have moved your head according to the report I have here from Mr. Croteau. Do you remember Mr. Croteau?"

Rachel opened her eyes half way and tilted the large breasts at a dangerous angle. She smiled.

"I'm pleased to see you smile," said the fat lips. Rachel raised her eyes to the black moon face. The fat lips were smiling. Rachel straightened her head to level so the large breasts could settle at an even keel. "I think the medications are finally wearing off." A plump black hand wrote something on a yellow sheet inside the manila file folder. "I will look forward to seeing you tomorrow, Rachel."

***

Pearl Whitman entered the small room like a large ship sailing into port. She wore her kinky black hair pulled severely back into a stylish knot at the back of her head. Her gold earrings sat like jewels in the black velvet of her earlobes, bringing attention to the gold linked chain around her thick neck. She wore a silky blouse, white as a nun's wimple, and a fine navy blue gabardine skirt. Her black skin glistened in the warm room like ebony on a misty morning. Suddenly the room felt full to overflowing.

"Good morning," Pearl said, taking a seat behind the small desk and beaming a pleasant smile around to the small group. She made herself comfortable, opened a file and began to read. "We have Rachel's family, Floyd, Willa, and Enoch, but not Jessie. Where's Jessie?" She raised her head and glanced around.

"Her lawyer has restricted her attendance," Enoch said.

"Humph. We have Detective Joseph D'nardo, Attorney Christopher Gallagher, and," she looked up and said, "I guess that's it." She leafed through some legal documents in another folder and cleared her throat.

Willa was already crying. Pearl looked at Willa then reached behind her to snatch some tissues from a box sitting on an old radiator. Willa took the tissues and wiped her nose then crumpled them in her trembling hands. Enoch slipped his arm around his mother's shoulders and gave her a supportive hug.

"At the request of our senior psychiatrist, I am taking over the case of Mrs. Rachel Vogel," Pearl began, locking her black eyes on each person as she moved her gaze around the circle. "My caseload is double the recommended number, not that I'm complaining, but Rachel is a most challenging case and there is great urgency in achieving her recovery according to these

99

documents." She pulled two sheets of paper out and spread them on the desk. "She's the key witness to a murder in one case. She's the prime suspect in another case. Quite a lot for one person with a frail mind to handle." Pearl returned the papers to the folder. "So, here is what I have to report today.

"I see that you, Floyd Keller, her father, have had yourself appointed guardian. You," she looked at Enoch, dressed in his uniform and still holding his mother, "appear to have appointed yourself as her chief protector. I trust you'll tell me why in session. Mrs. Keller?" Pearl looked at Willa with a kind and inquisitive expression. "You have two daughters in great trouble. I'm sure all of this is most distressing for you." Willa resumed weeping.

Pearl looked at Attorney Gallagher. "Your interests will be served if Rachel recovers enough to be competent (as defined in a court of law) to stand trial. For the time being, I would ask that you bide your time. Perhaps you would call me in six or eight weeks. At that time I will be better able to give you a progress report.

"And Detective D'nardo." Pearl shifted her steady gaze to Joe's face then pulled a letter from the folder. "I have a letter from the District Attorney's office reminding me that Mrs. Vogel is a vital witness to a murder case and that her recovery is of the utmost importance, and that time is of the essence."

Pearl stared at Joe, not even blinking those large black eyes with the startling white edges. "What is of the essence here, Mr. D'nardo, is the mental and emotional health of Mrs. Rachel Vogel." More kindly and with a slight deflation in her chest and shoulders, Pearl continued. "I also understand that Rachel's sister will stand trial for murder and that you and the District Attorney believe Rachel's testimony has significant bearing on the event. If you will be patient with the therapeutic process, I will be patient with your concerns. You may call me in four weeks for a progress report. Other than that, I don't want to hear from you."

Joe cleared his throat and said, "Ms. Whitman. I brought Mrs.

Vogel's glasses. From the looks of them it appears she will need them when she gets better."

"Thank you, Detective." Pearl put the eyeglasses case in a side drawer and tucked the letter back into the file.

"If you two," she looked at Gallagher and D'nardo, "will kindly excuse us, I'd like to talk to Rachel's family in private."

The two men rose, thanked Ms. Whitman, and left the room.

"Now," Pearl said a bit more expansively. "I have a problem." She studied each family member for a moment and said, "I have a patient who doesn't speak. The reports from the ward supervisor confirm she appears catatonic, showing no interest in herself or anyone around her. She needs to be fed, bathed and clothed. I need to observe her in her natural state so I have taken her off all the medications she was on initially."

"I knew they would pump her full of drugs," Willa cried. "Did they restrain her? Was she locked in her room?"

"No, Mrs. Keller. She gave no cause for restraint, and most patients, as docile as she, are assigned to wards. She is fine." Pearl waited a moment for Willa to absorb her comforting words.

"I have met with Rachel three times in the past week. Though she does not speak with me yet, I believe she will. I believe she has suffered a severe shock, but I need to know more about her life prior to the death of her husband. It is hard for me to determine how great an effect that incident had on her, versus, an accumulation of prior incidents in her life, adulthood or childhood."

"She had a very normal and healthy childhood," Floyd said, gripping his Bible in both hands. "You won't find anything in her early years to contribute to a psychotic condition."

"I'm glad to hear that," Pearl said. "What I want to say this morning is, my ability to work with Rachel will depend on my ability to learn about her life from her family. With that pool of knowledge, I will be better equipped to assess her responses and perhaps achieve progress more rapidly." Pearl tucked her folders into the briefcase she'd sat on the floor beside her.

"As an aside, for me, time is also of the essence. I find Rachel's case compelling, but I am three months pregnant and will be going out on maternity leave in five months. I hope you all will cooperate with me." Pearl rose and turned toward the door, opening it and holding it for the others to exit. As the family members passed by her, Pearl suddenly got an idea.

"Officer Keller, could I please see you for a moment?" She put her briefcase on the desk and extracted a pen and note pad. "Would you kindly give me the name of Jessie's lawyer? I would like to try to include Jessie in gathering Rachel's background story."

CHAPTER 12

Confessions

"You're very persistent," Jessie said to Detective D'nardo as she took a seat in the dark corner of the library-like bar and lounge in a town north of Boston. Floor-to-ceiling bookcases lined two walls conveying a sense of richness and well-being. Orange and purple rays of lingering sunlight dropped slowly behind a stand of trees that separated the restaurant from the two-lane highway running from Key West, Florida to Fort Kent, Maine. It was the first Saturday in August. "That's usually my job."

Jessie dropped her pack of Virginia Slims on the table and stuck a cigarette between her lips. Joe took the BIC lighter from Jessie's hand and lit her cigarette for her. "Just like old-fashioned courtesy in the movies." She smiled at Joe. "Crown Royal on the rocks," she said to the waitress.

"Cutty, neat," Joe said. "Persistence pays off." He flashed a crooked grin.

"Sorry to keep you waiting. Been here long?" Jessie asked.

"No. I did have time to study that artsy interpretation of the Morton Salt girl," he said, indicating a framed poster of a young woman holding an open umbrella. The only rain in the picture was falling from underneath the umbrella. He looked around the shadowy lounge. "Come here often?"

"No. But it's a good place for furtive gatherings." Jessie rolled her eyes mysteriously and chuckled softly. "My lawyer will kill me if he finds out."

The waitress delivered their drinks. "Help yourself to the cheese and crackers," she suggested, pointing to an alcove near the bar.

"Don't bother," Jessie said as soon as the waitress was out of hearing. "The cheese is recycled wallpaper paste." She lifted an eyebrow at Joe and said, "So?"

Joe raised his drink and motioned for a toast. "Here's to proving you are the biggest liar I've ever met."

"I won't dignify that with a response." Jessie sipped her whiskey. The whiskey's first sharp bite made her shiver. "On the phone you swore we would not discuss the case." She gave him a quirky smile and said, "Now that I've revealed my secret trysting place, tell me why I'm here."

"I have a story idea," Joe said. He glanced around the smoky room. Small tables with chattering people filled two-thirds of the large room while a packed bar took up the other third, its tall stools squashed together while additional imbibers stood, two layers deep. "I thought since you'd been shunted away from the top stories, locked in the closet as you said, that you might like to write a little human-interest story."

"Christ," Jessie said with disgust. "My editor won't even let me cover the obits. Said I could either lay low with a paycheck or take a vacation without."

"So why not write a story about an attractive young news reporter who takes the rap for her brother-in-law's death to save her mentally fragile sister? She thinks she's clever and can get off with the claim of self-defense."

Jessie shot Joe a hateful glance but listened.

"This reporter makes up this fat lie, even taking notes on her own fabrication, and thinks she can fool the cops and her own lawyer. " Jessie opened her mouth to speak; Joe held up his hand to silence her. "But, one guy doesn't buy it. There's a detective who thinks the story's a bunch of bunk. And—" He held up his hand again. "Let me finish. This detective would like to close out the investigation, like his superior is demanding, but he can't.

Not only is he concerned about a miscarriage of justice, though the reporter is hell-bent on self-destruction, he's taken a liking to the reporter. With the way she treats him, he looks like a fool." Joe glared at Jessie over the edge of his glass and sipped his Scotch. "But he's not."

Jessie leaned her chin on her hand and studied Joe's face for some time. She stubbed her cigarette out and said, "I'm hungry. Can we order now?"

After the waitress lit the stubby oil lamp and arranged their place mats and silverware, Jessie responded, looking at Joe and revealing a new shade of softness in her face.

"You are wrong with your version of the story, but there are some things you don't know."

"I'd like to learn." Joe signaled for another round of drinks. "There's a lot about you I'd like to know."

Jessie's expression became more solemn as she sat back in the wooden captain's chair and rested her hands in her lap.

"I am responsible for the death of Rachel's husband. I am also responsible for her marriage to him."

"I thought Enoch introduced them. He and Butch served in Vietnam together."

"That's true. Enoch did introduce them. I was fifteen at the time and even I knew they got married too quickly. Rachel never met Butch's parents, well not his father. His mother was already dead by then. Rachel acted like it was a whirlwind romance, right out of a cheap novel, which, by the way, I found she liked to read. Books like that were forbidden in our home. When she got married and moved out to live with Butch, I went through some boxes she'd left behind in our attic, sealed with tape and marked, *Keep Out*."

"Doesn't that mean, *Keep Out*?" Joe asked.

"In media-speak, that means, *Open Me*." Jessie laughed. "It wasn't that I was shocked to find her stash of books—I figured I'd snitch them, one at a time, and read them by flashlight under the covers. I was surprised to learn that she even thought about romance." Jessie paused and grimaced. "I know that's a cruel thing to say, but Rachel wasn't like other girls, talking about boys and going out on dates. Mind you, she was six years older and acted more like a second mother with me than a sister. We never lay on our beds at night and shared secrets. By the time she left, I was too young to date and she was in her last semester of college and married."

"Anything else of interest in the box?" Joe asked.

"Not that I'm telling you," Jessie said. "Anyway, Rachel never dated anyone until she met Butch. That is, except for one fellow who used to come to visit with Father because he wanted to become a minister when he grew up. His name was Jeremy, Jeremy Blaisdell I think. Rachel was sixteen and would always be busy when Jeremy came to talk with Father. After a few visits, Jeremy would make a point of exiting the house along a route where he thought he would encounter Rachel. If she was sweeping the front porch, she would pretend she didn't see him. If he stopped by the kitchen, she would keep ironing, head down, until he made her acknowledge his presence.

"Father didn't complain about the increasing time that Jeremy took to chat with Rachel after each visit. They both attended religious academy, he one grade ahead of Rachel. Rachel never received attention from any of the other boys. It wasn't that she was ugly; you can see she isn't. Kids are cruel and though her eyes had partially receded over the years, and the thickness of her lenses had decreased with better optical techniques, she was a wallflower."

The slim waitress in clunky-heeled shoes slipped their meals in front of them and hurried away.

"When Jeremy asked Rachel to attend a basketball game with him, Mother cried. You'd have thought Rachel was going to the prom, though the C.R.O.W.s don't do proms. They think dancing is filthy and lascivious. Then Jeremy began sitting with Rachel in church. That's next to marriage in that religion. Such a public declaration.

"Well, like I told you I was only ten. I was reaching my literary peak, so I thought."

"You'd better take a break and eat something," Joe said. "You'll pass out from hunger and I won't hear the rest of the story."

Getting her small mouth around the huge cheeseburger wasn't easy, but Jessie gave it a valiant try. Juice from the meat and dressing oozed onto her hands while the rich aroma of grilled beef with sautéed mushrooms and onions filled her nostrils.

"Christ!" Jessie said, "I'm going to need a shower after this meal. I forgot how fat they make their burgers here."

Jessie ate hungrily then laid the remainder of her disfigured burger on her plate, wiped her hands on a wad of napkins and continued.

"I was in my plagiarism phase back then and also had honed my skulking skills to a fine art, including skipping out to visit friends whose parents weren't quite so strict as mine. So, one afternoon I went to my friend Sylvia's house, and watched a movie on TV, unedited." Jessie drew her mouth into an exaggerated 'O' of surprise and opened her eyes wide. "Sinful, movies, sex, lust, evil." She laughed. "When the C.R.O.W.s showed Pat Boone movies at Recovery University, they edited the frigging things. Can you believe it? Editing Pat Boone? He was the original sanctified priss of Hollywood." Jessie took another bite of her smooshed burger, this time attacking it with a knife and fork.

"The movie Sylvia and I saw was *A Summer Place* with Tab Hunter and Sandra Dee. Oh my god, was Tab Hunter gorgeous! I fantasized about him for days, hating Sandra Dee, reveling in the tragic story of star-crossed lovers, and hating their parents." Jessie stopped for breath and finished her whiskey. "Ugh, that tastes horrible with hamburger." She took a few more bites of her food then pushed her plate away from her.

"So," Jessie continued, leaning back and taking on a more sober expression, "I decided to write a similar story with minor revisions, you know, because we didn't have a beach nearby and all. I used the same plot replacing Tab Hunter and Sandra Dee with Rachel and Jeremy. I had to change the location of their illicit sexual encounter to the basement of our church, but the story hung together nicely and I thought it was terrific. As was my habit with my best stories, I always took them to school and shared them with Sylvia. That morning, I'd laid my pages of precious scribbling on the table under my lunch bag. When Father yelled for me to hurry—he drove me over to the school every morning—I grabbed my lunch and forgot the story." Jessie paused. "I'll be right back." She hurried to the ladies' room and returned quickly.

Joe had finished his dinner and was sipping his drink.

"I needed a bath after that hamburger," she said, resettling herself in her chair. "So, the essence of the story is; Mother found my story and showed it to Father. Jeremy was forbidden to enter our home again and told to stay away from Rachel in school, and, they took Rachel to a doctor for an examination. Rachel screamed so loudly when the doctor tried to examine her, the doctor refused to proceed."

"Didn't you tell them it was all a lie?" Joe cried, leaning across his dirty plate, his eyes tearing with concern. "My lord, Jessie. It was a pack of lies! Right?"

"I told Father I'd made it all up. But I couldn't admit I'd seen a movie at a friend's house. Father called me into his study and yelled at me for trying to cover up for my sister. He said it was bad enough for me to be sneaking around and watching other people. But he knew the truth when he saw it, and spanked me for trying to protect Rachel. 'No ten-year-old could make up a story like that,' he'd said. 'You'd have to have seen it with your own eyes.'" Joe relaxed a bit and leaned back in his chair to listen. "He said he was sure that if he searched for witnesses, he could find them, but he didn't want to shame the family in front of the whole church. So he gave me one of his index cards with a Bible verse from Matthew 19, verse 18. I'll never forget it as long as I live. It said, 'Thou shalt not bear false witness.' I had to write it out one hundred times and bring the papers to my father."

Joe laughed. "That's worse than saying the rosary over and over."

"I hated the spankings. But more than having my bottom burned fiery red—*I hated having to kiss his hand afterwards, but no fucking way am I telling Joe that*—I hated writing out those Bible verses." She laughed with Joe. "He made all of us do that in payment for our sins until we reached college age." She looked at Joe in resignation. "You know, and I don't know why I'm telling you this, but, the Bible teaches us to love our mother and our father, to honor them and respect them. I've never loved my father. I feared him, and avoided him, but never loved."

"And Rachel?" Joe asked. "What about Rachel? Did she love him?"

"God only knows. If I'm honest about my memories, I guess she loved him. She did everything he ever told her to do. She waited on him hand and foot when mother was too sad to come out of her room. She went along with everything they demanded: no boys, lots of housework, and silence. God, our home was as silent as a saloon in a ghost town."

Joe asked for the check.

"I've got an early ride down to the State Police Crime Lab in the morning. I wish I could drive you back to Boston and say good night there, but you were the one who insisted we meet here."

They rose from their chairs and headed slowly for the door.

"Another time?" Joe asked as they approached her car. "I promise I won't discuss the case."

"Maybe," Jessie said turning to her car and leaning against the window to scan the interior before turning the lock.

"Looks like you know a few safety precautions," Joe said. "That's good. I'll call you in a few days." Then he added softly, "Thank you for seeing me."

Jessie scanned the parked cars as she exited the restaurant parking lot, imagining that every patron was a spy for her lawyer.

She turned on the radio as she proceeded south on US Route 1 and tried to relax. Being with Detective D'nardo left her feeling edgy. Oh, hell, she told herself, Levine will never know. And frankly, Joe wasn't bad company. And, more than ever, she needed Joe to believe her story.

She tuned in a Boston rock station and thought about the things she hadn't told him: the details of her father's punishments and the fight she and Rachel had had that still haunted her in her quiet moments. She passed a darkened auto auction lot next to a comedy nightclub. *Not much comedy in my life at the moment. And certainly none for Rachel.* She shifted her thoughts to her visit at the state hospital. *Glad I don't cover the health beat. I'd heard that place was ghoulish. Never thought in my wildest dreams I'd visit a family member locked up there.*

She passed *The Ship*, a restaurant fashioned like an eighteenth century frigate. It appeared to have run aground twenty miles inland, its masts still rigged but its decks illuminated by electricity from a later century.

She let her memory drift back further, back to that Christmas in 1964 when she'd been fourteen and had a mean mouth. Rachel was a junior in college and had been giving her motherly advice about wearing too much makeup.

"I can't believe Father lets you get away with any makeup at your age." Rachel continued washing the dishes while Jessie rinsed and wiped. "I wasn't allowed to wear makeup, at all, until I was eighteen. Not until I graduated high school."

"Just call me Jezebel," Jessie told Rachel. "And throw me to the dogs." She gave Rachel a devilish grin and stacked the plates back in the high cupboard.

"Yes, I know, your namesake." Rachel let the water out of the sink and dried her hands on a towel. "She was a very bad woman. I would think you could choose a far better example to emulate." Rachel untied the strings of her apron and hung it on a hook near the back door. "If you plaster on your makeup and dress provocatively, you look cheap, like you're chasing after men."

"You should try it," Jessie said. "At the rate you're going, that's the only way you're going to get a man." She slammed the silverware drawer shut. "Frankly, you could used some makeup and a whole lot more." Rachel's crushed expression stopped the flow of Jessie's words. "Well, I didn't mean to hurt your feelings, Rachel. Honestly, you act like you don't even want a date, much less a husband."

"That isn't true," Rachel said, looking furtively toward the living room in case either parent was approaching the kitchen. "I do want a husband, very badly."

"In that case," Jessie had said as Rachel helped put the rest of the glasses in the cupboard, "you'd better grab the first warm body that comes within reach or you're going to be an old maid."

Jessie's thoughts returned to the present as she passed a billboard mounted on top of a red clapboard house on the outskirts of Chelsea. A brightly lit image of Jesus Christ loomed against the night sky. His hand was raised in a blessing. It read, *Jesus Saves.* "Right," Jessie said softly. "Tell poor Rachel that."

CHAPTER 13

Orchards of Memory

Pearl guided Willa to a seat in a comfortable plastic chair with wooden arms next to her battered desk. "I'm glad you could come Mrs. Keller," Pearl said. "I'm sure it took a great deal of courage."

"You said I could help Rachel. I had no choice." Willa looked up furtively then down at her lap. "Floyd wouldn't drive me. I had to ask Enoch."

"Was Floyd upset that you came?"

"He said I'd regret it. He said he'd told you everything you needed to know, but if I insisted, I could walk."

Pearl took in the scattered strands of graying hair on Willa's bowed head and decided to change the subject. "Well, I appreciate your coming. I do believe you can help Rachel." Willa looked up with her eyes and slowly raised her head.

"Rachel and I meet two or three times during the week but since she hasn't spoken yet, I would like to hear your perspective on her childhood. Perhaps you can tell me what she was like when she was little, what made her happy, what made her sad. How you interacted with her."

"Me? Why me? I thought you just wanted to talk about Rachel. You always attack the mother." Willa started to cry. Pearl handed her some tissues. "Floyd warned me. He said you people always blame the mothers. He said if I came here you would lock me up and torture me." Her voice became clogged and squeaky with emotion. "He told me you would drug me and chain me to my

112

bed, leave me screaming in the night, high in a tower where no one could hear me." She bowed her head into her hands and her shoulders trembled.

"Mrs. Keller," Pearl said as she handed Willa the box of tissues. "If you are going to help your daughter, you really must get a hold on yourself." She waited while Willa sniffed and blew her nose hard. She studied Willa's dress, clean and neatly ironed though it bespoke a taste for modesty that crossed the line of fashion into frumpiness. In a way, Pearl thought, it fit Willa perfectly. She wore no makeup or lipstick and her thin straight bangs, reminiscent of an old Bette Davis movie, completed her scraggly '40s look.

Willa refused to look up at Pearl. "I hear your fears of mental institutions," Pearl said. "Indeed, this facility is a sad place. Just look around you. You can see the peeling paint, the outbuildings falling into disrepair. We've got a deplorable mix of patients, some truly psychotic, most just lost souls who were hurt and never loved. But, we don't torture anyone. Restraints are used only in extreme cases. I'm sure you're imagining padded rooms, but they are few and far between. Why it's almost impossible to get a reservation these days."

Pearl's attempt at humor was not totally wasted. Willa looked up and gulped back her sobs. I hope I'm right, Pearl thought to herself. She may be overly dramatic and accustomed to playing the victim, but I'm thinking that honesty, kindness and a dose of straight talk in an emotionally safe environment, might create a shortcut through Willa's fears.

Like a child testing the hot water in a steaming tub, Willa put forth a small feeler. "I haven't always felt well," she said.

"Have you been ill?"

"No. I just don't feel well a lot of the time. When I got married I promised to be the perfect minister's wife and the best mother, and play the organ and teach piano lessons, and keep a clean home, and…"

"I'm sure you did it all, but at a cost," Pearl said. "Today we call it Superwoman. We say it with a sense of humor. No one can achieve all those things and stay on the outside." She spread her large black arms out wide to encompass the whole institution. "On the other hand, who can resist all this?" She smiled warmly at Willa and said, "I'm sure you were a good mother to Rachel. I'm sure you were, and are, a good wife."

As Pearl's kind words flowed into Willa's starved soul, Willa's painful expression melted like carved chocolate in the hot sun. Her features crumbled and she burst into tears. "No. No. I'm not." She fluttered her hands futilely then grabbed fresh tissues. "I'm a failure. Look how I've failed my children, poor Rachel, poor Jessie. I'm a horrible wife." She covered her eyes with wads of tissues and then dropped her hands. The suffering and self-hatred in her eyes seemed to flow out in her tears as she looked at Pearl and pled for understanding. "My husband hates me. He's never loved me. He sees me as a stupid, wanton woman. It's Rachel he loved, not me. Now he doesn't even love her. He hasn't loved her since her eyes got big." Willa looked at Pearl, gulped back her tears and spoke in a lower voice. "Since she stopped being beautiful; when he used to take her everywhere with him." She swiped at her tears again. "They were inseparable, until, that is, until her eyes bugged out."

"Willa," Pearl said. "May I call you that?"

"Yes," Willa said. "I'd like that."

"Take a deep breath and sit back. Try to relax. Now, tell me about Rachel, when she was little, before she contracted the thyroid disease."

Willa gave her nose one last vigorous wipe, put her shoulders back a little and said, "Rachel was an angel. She was born three years after Enoch. Before she came, little Enoch and I had made a life together, with his father being away in seminary and all; it was just Enoch and me. We lived with Floyd's parents at the time; it was the war and all, but I felt it was just Enoch and me. Then

Floyd came home and we moved to Cleveland, our first home together, small but nice, right across the street from the church. Then in September of '44, Rachel was born. She was a tiny, blue-eyed, blond-haired angel, well, until her blue eyes turned green. It'd been a difficult birth but she still looked like she'd come straight from heaven. Floyd thought so, too." Willa looked around the small room as though someone might be in a corner listening.

"Floyd hadn't shown much interest in Enoch, being away so much and Enoch growing up without him. Floyd loved little Rachel, holding her and rocking her to sleep after her evening feeding. I'd watch him from the kitchen doorway and breath a silent prayer of thanks to the Lord for such a good father."

"And husband?" Pearl prompted.

"He was a wonderful husband." Willa spoke more rapidly. "Any problems he might have mentioned were my fault. He always explained what I'd done wrong so I could understand that." More slowly she said, "But he loved Rachel. From the time he could take Rachel out, you know, when she was two or three, visiting a sick person, running errands, he took her with him. I remember at church picnics, I'd be busy with food and serving and cleanup and I wouldn't have to think a moment about little Rachel. Floyd would walk around and chat with everyone; everyone loved Floyd. He'd carry Rachel on his shoulders like a golden angel perched above the crowd."

"What about Enoch, during the picnics?"

"Oh, Enoch was stuck to me like a burdock," Willa said with a wistful look on her face. "Enoch was the sweetest, most obedient child. Every night he would sit and listen to a Bible story and beg for more. He looked up to his father, and knew he wanted to be a minister when he was only ten years old."

"I thought Enoch—you do only have one son, correct? I thought Enoch was a police officer."

"The Enoch you see now is a police officer. But he went to the seminary and he was a minister, like his father." A look of pride flashed briefly over Willa's tear-stained face. Then her sad expression returned. "He lost his faith when he learned that his wife had been unfaithful to him. Then he became a police officer." A look of longing came over Willa's face and tears filled her eyes. "It was such a lovely wedding. Leah was a beautiful girl. He loved her so much. He'd saved himself for her, you know."

"Do you mean he was a virgin on his wedding night?"

"Yes." Willa sighed with deep sadness.

"So when did Rachel have her first incident with thyroid?" Pearl asked. "It appears to be a focal point in the family."

"It wasn't my fault," Willa said. "No one could say exactly when it started. It just happened." She looked at Pearl with pleading eyes. "Floyd thought I should have taken better care of her. I don't know what I could have done to prevent it. I did my best. And he's the only other person who watched over her. When I went to the church to practice with the choir in the evenings, I'd make sure the supper was cleared and dishes washed and everything was tidied up. Then I'd ask Floyd to read a story to Enoch and Rachel, though by then they liked different stories, and then put them to bed." Willa paused. "I was doing the Lord's business too, playing the organ and supporting the choir. Floyd knew that."

Willa stopped speaking and let her gaze wander to the large windows like she hadn't noticed them before. She looked back at Pearl and resumed in a less defensive tone. "When Rachel was little she was so tenderhearted. She loved animals. Used to bring home every stray cat or dog she found. She'd help me bandage their wounds, insisting that she daub them with the Merthiolate, though it always stung so badly. She'd croon to them and tell them that everything would be better when they grew up." Willa lifted her shoulders and straightened her back.

"I always had to take them to the shelter. We couldn't have animals in the house, what with all the work I had to do and church members stopping by with no advance notice. One thing I remember clearly was, Rachel became very unhappy when she

116

learned the story of Noah and the Ark. The first time she heard that story, she cried. It was in Sabbath school class, you know, Sabbath morning in church before the sermon. The children's class instructor sent her assistant up to get me in the sanctuary. I ran downstairs and there was Rachel, inconsolable. At five years old, she understood that when Noah took the animals into the ark, two by two, that all the other animals on earth had drowned in the flood." Again Willa swiped her nose with her soiled tissues. "That's the first time I ever lied." Willa looked up at Pearl, her eyes begging forgiveness as she confessed. "It's the only time I ever lied. I told Rachel that Jesus had found a safe place on earth, high up in a range of mountains on the other side of the big sea, and made a game preserve for the other animals so they would be safe. That made her feel better."

"Do you love your husband, Willa?" Pearl asked changing the subject quickly, not giving Willa time to consider.

"Of course I love my husband!" Willa said somewhat curtly. "What kind of Christian woman doesn't love her husband, especially Floyd? He's so handsome and so dedicated to God's work. Why I've worshiped him, I mean," she said a bit flustered, "not worshiped him, like you worship the Lord, but I've loved him and been devoted to him since the day our parents said we had to get married."

"Had to get married?" Pearl leaned closer over her desk, confused at what she'd heard. In the kindest of tones she asked, "Were you pregnant before the wedding?"

"No!" Willa cried, jumping back and letting her voice rise to a thin screech. "No. He'd never touched me. He'd never even spoken to me, hardly, except for our ride home from college and that time we spent on the bus. He'd hardly known I existed until we got married."

"Please tell me about your courtship," Pearl said, settling back into her chair.

***

Willa had left half an hour ago, and Pearl found herself wandering about in the old orchard, now just a few knobby trees, twisted and broken by age and neglect. She knew from the history of the institution that this had once been a lovely orchard where inmates had cultivated apple, cherry and peach trees, bringing in the fruits of their labors to the vast kitchens for the cooks to bake huge trays of cobbler and shortcake.

Pearl broke off a drooping twig from a tree and whipped it through the air. Lord almighty, she said to herself. How Rachel's parents' two stories differed. Sometimes, she laughed to herself, it's like Dumpster-diving in the dark, hoping to find a diamond ring in a slimy corner.

Poor Willa, as Pearl had come to view Mrs. Keller, was a most frightened bird. She flopped around like her wings were broken and her tiny claws crippled. Sadness and disappointment had overshadowed her life leaving her feathers dull and without luster. But the more that Pearl learned about Willa, the more she believed in Willa's potential.

As was often the case in Pearl's experience, those who seemed the most frightened and the most vulnerable, were the ones who hid a deep well of courage inside, out of reach of their own psyche. Nature had given them a built-in resiliency to which they were not privy until life forced them up against it. There was an internal rescue system, but it took a certain crisis to pull back the curtain and reveal the power.

There must be a reason why Floyd had tried to throw Pearl off Willa's track. They didn't seem to parent as a team. It was clearly Floyd who appeared more involved and concerned about Rachel. He'd insisted Pearl should talk with him, not Willa, to learn about his daughter's childhood and upbringing.

"You should meet with me first," he'd said when she'd called them on the phone. "After all, the study of human nature and the human condition is my profession too. I'm nothing if not astute in dealing with the failings of mankind, though, I wouldn't say that Rachel has many failings. Perhaps she did rush into her marriage with Butch, but we can discuss that at length when I meet with you at your office. I'll be available when it fits your schedule."

Pearl whipped the peach twig through the air more vigorously at the memory of her meeting with Floyd.

Talking with Floyd had felt more like a military debriefing than the sharing of information about a daughter by a loving father. Pearl fully understood that a therapist should always be in charge of a session. But there had been times in her experience when she'd gone with the flow and let the interviewee take charge, telling her more about themselves in the unstructured conversation than she could have gleaned with all the proper questions. Pearl was also careful to form conclusions slowly. For now, Floyd was more of a question than an answer. Plus, and in direct conflict with her professional code, Pearl had her preferences in personality types she didn't love working with. Bible-carrying-men-of-god was near the top of her list. She'd needed to keep a close watch over her own feelings with this one.

Yes, she continued her ruminations as she looked down the slope beyond the fruit trees, something was wrong with the Keller family story. Something was terribly wrong but she hadn't yet found a clue, not one clue, after hours of talking with Floyd, Willa, and Enoch.

Jessie still remained out of her reach. Was that significant? She didn't know. Sisters could have strange and convoluted relationships, keep secrets, protect each other or destroy each other. Which applied to Rachel and Jessie?

"Now there's a puzzle," Pearl said out loud. Pearl looked at her watch and cried out loud again, "Oh my god. Oh my god. I'm so late." Stupid to be late with a group session filled with paranoid crazies, she chided herself silently. Already they believed the world was aligned against them. If she came late, they'd think she didn't like them either. Pearl hustled her sturdy legs, turning an ankle and nearly falling as she ran.

For a foolish tired moment she fantasized about sitting on a couch, her leg propped on a stool, her crutches nearby, and unable to go to work or even do her own housework. Hmmm.

Lord, she exclaimed to herself as she hobbled over the uneven ground. I must be exhausted to fantasize having my foot in a cast to get some rest. She laughed at herself and limped up the steps of the Women's Wing, sweat trickling down her temples. I'll take a break when the baby comes.

CHAPTER 14

Close the Curtain

"Sit down, Joe." Detective D'nardo dropped into a chair in Lieutenant Tinker's office. The dog days of summer had wilted every dusty plant in the cluttered offices, and every officer in the stifling building. Lt. Tinker tossed a tri-folded piece of paper across his desk. "Wrap it up, Joe," he said. "Game's over. That crazy witness of yours isn't going to testify."

Joe leaned forward and took the typewritten letter and read it slowly. Much of the wording was jargon, known only to the inner circles of the psychiatric and mental health profession. But he got the bottom line.

"Though patient-therapist confidentiality precludes me from detailing Mrs. Rachel Vogel's condition, I do not believe she will be ready to testify in a reasonable amount of time, if ever. We have taken her off medication and are treating her as a shock victim. That means we do not see her as having psychotic tendencies. She has begun to speak but only in the most limited of terms. My professional opinion is that even if her rate of recovery improves, she may never remember the incident of July 11, 1976 when her husband was killed. Therefore I do not foresee her playing a probative role in the case against Ms. Jessie Keller.

"I am sorry I could not be more hopeful. The mind is always a mystery and we discover its secrets, one day at a time."

"Shit," Joe said. "There's got to be another way. What about reverse shock therapy? You know, jolting the person back into memory." Tinker snickered at Joe. "What I'm thinking is," Joe continued, standing and pacing around the tiny office, "is what about hypnosis? Don't they use hypnosis to make a person recall things they've buried so deep they could never recall them on their own?" Joe kicked a dusty old typewriter on the floor in the corner and took a sharp U-turn. "What about getting a big-time psychiatrist? Boston's loaded with the mucky-mucks of medicine. Why not ask one of those guys to take her case pro bono; request another evaluation? We could tell them it's going to be a high profile case, might give them a bigger name."

"Maybe Larry Glick will perform hypnosis on her, take her back to kindergarten, tell us how long she was breast-fed." Tinker's sarcastic mention of the famous Boston talk radio host underscored his frustration. "Sit down, Joe," the lieutenant said again. "You know the state's already paid the freight for everything Mrs. Vogel has coming to her under the law."

"How about using her own assets? She and her husband own that two-family house."

"You know her assets have been frozen by that petition her employer's lawyer processed. Hell." Tinker laughed and put his feet on his desk. "If I were Rachel Vogel and knew you wanted to pin my husband's murder on me, that my ex-employer was charging me with embezzlement, and you wanted me to confess that I'd been physically abused by my husband, I'd probably want to stay right at Danvers State and play with the cuckoos." Tinker dropped his feet to the floor.

"Give it up, Joe." He stood up and came around his desk, shoved a stack of overflowing file baskets to the side and sat on the dusty front edge. More seriously he said, "We know you're a good detective, the best. You've done everything in your power to investigate this case and make sure the correct suspect is charged." Tinker slid off his desk and began pacing. "Let's face it Joe; I can't hold off on this any longer. I've got hot cases that are going cold while you chase a hunch. For Christ sakes, you've got a dead body, the murder weapon with the suspect's fingerprints confirmed, a signed confession and motive. What in hell more do you want?" Tinker turned to Joe and laughed. "I know the traditional answer is, 'A signed confession.' You've got that. Give it up. Take the files over to the DA this afternoon. I'll call him and tell him to expect you. Case closed."

Joe exited Tinker's office, slamming the door behind him. He turned back quickly, opened the door, stuck his head in and said, "Sorry,"

"Leave it open," Tinker said. "Buy you a beer after work?"

Joe went into his own cramped office he shared with another detective. He grabbed a stack of files from the corner of his desk and plopped them down in the center of his associate's desk.

"Tinker make you close the Vogel investigation?" his associate asked.

"Yeah," Joe said. "That black shrink says she doesn't think Rachel will ever recall the incident of her husband's death, even if she does recover." Joe grabbed a thick folder off the file cabinet behind him and headed out the door. "Flip through those cases and pick the three hottest. We'll work on them when I get back."

CHAPTER 15

Scribes and Pharisees

Pearl jerked her head up as Floyd burst into her office unannounced. "Good afternoon, Mr. Keller."

"What do you mean, inviting Willa to meet with you again? I thought all you needed were a couple of interviews with her. You've had them. You're done." Floyd took a threatening stance, looming over Pearl's cluttered desk, his battered Bible clutched tightly in his right hand. "If I want Willa in an insane asylum, I'll have her committed myself!"

"I've no doubt of that, Mr. Keller," Pearl said with a straight face. "Would you like to sit down and calm down?" Pearl motioned to a chair. "Or do you prefer restraints?" Pearl flashed a disarming smile and glanced down at his Bible.

"You don't talk like that to me," Floyd said, calming himself and making an attempt at civility. "I'm a minister." He took a small step backwards. "I deserve your respect."

"Please have a seat." Pearl indicated the chair near her desk. "Perhaps I could get you a cup of coffee, or a soda?"

"I don't drink coffee. I'm fine thank you." Floyd sat down but remained poised to rise.

"Your wife needs help," Pearl said in a calm, matter-of-fact voice, observing his puritanical appearance in his dark gray suit and brilliant white dress shirt. "I believe she can help me and I can help her as I work with Rachel."

"There's nothing wrong with Willa that a little backbone and an end to her sniveling wouldn't cure. She's fine. Plays her organ all day long. She no longer has to fulfill the duties she once did as a minister's wife because I'm a Vice President and work in Administration now. She can sit at home and do almost nothing. Her life's a bed of roses." He spoke more slowly as his initial flare of anger dissipated. "She couldn't ask for better." He glanced out of the windows to the distance then back at Pearl. "She never was much for the public eye and now, all she has to do is keep the house clean and cook my meals."

"What about the stress of having one daughter institutionalized and the other daughter indicted for murder? What about the tragedy in her son's life, though he appears to have a good grip. I wouldn't call Willa's life a bed of roses."

"Frankly, I wouldn't call Willa's life any of your business." Floyd gave Pearl a dismissive shake of his head. In a slightly more conciliatory tone he said, "From a traditional viewpoint, she's got a good life, nothing to worry about. You don't need to waste your time on her. I've always taken good care of her." Floyd slid back in his chair a few inches.

"What was it you wanted to discuss with me?" Pearl asked. "I have an appointment shortly."

"Just that." Floyd shifted his Bible to his left hand and struck a firm pose. The tensing of the muscles in his jaw matched the bellicose look in his eyes. "I came to tell you that Willa does not need therapy. One family member in a mental hospital is enough. I won't have it." He punctuated his words by tapping on Pearl's desk firmly with his right forefinger.

"Did you ever seriously discuss putting Willa in a mental institution?" Pearl asked.

"What are you suggesting?"

"It's a simple question. Have you ever discussed having Willa institutionalized?"

"No. Never!"

"Never, Mr. Keller? That's funny because I understand that Willa has had a few bouts of depression that caused you to express deep disappointment in her. She said you had mentioned institutionalization. Perhaps you were only kidding? She is obviously terrified of the concept. You can see that by her response to Rachel's situation."

"Willa's afraid of her own shadow." Floyd waved his hand in a dismissive gesture. "She's skittish. She cowers and hides in her room as a way to punish me for asking a few small things of her. Sometimes she abandons her faith in God and falls prey to the devil's temptations." Floyd cleared his throat and stood up. "She always recovers and returns to her deep love of Christ. She is a good Christian woman and knows her responsibilities." He paused then added, "And she doesn't need your shoulder to cry on. I can take care of her needs. I always have."

"Well," Pearl said, rising from her chair and walking toward her office door. "Thank you for coming by and expressing your concerns."

"Then you'll tell Willa she doesn't need a therapist?"

"No, I will not tell Willa that. Good-bye, Mr. Keller."

"You are stepping beyond the bounds of your authority."

"That would not be my preference," Pearl said. "I would deeply appreciate your cooperation. Good-bye, Mr. Keller."

***

Pearl left her office to get a fresh cup of coffee to ward off a slight chill in her bones though the mid-September day was still warm. Something about her encounters with Floyd Keller left her with the sense of a specter brushing past. She allowed a slight shiver to ripple through her body then sat down at her desk again and leaned back, heaving a sigh of relief. She gazed out the two long windows of her office that framed a beautiful vista of the distant town of Danvers. The expansive view was broken by a spread of woodlands on the other side of the wrought iron fence in the distance. The trees were resisting the change of autumn, still clinging to their summer green. *I still can't crack the code to Rachel's terror but perhaps a few more interviews with family members will help.* She grabbed Rachel's file and prepared her mind for the session ahead.

Funny how Mr. Keller had come in all riled up. Rather hostile for a man of God, she thought. She smiled to herself. An old Bible reference came to mind, one she had learned from her mother who was the most sincerely religious person Pearl had ever known. She continued letting her eyes rest as they scanned the treetops while she recalled the teachings of Jesus who saw the scribes and Pharisees for the hypocrites they were. "You strain at a gnat and swallow a camel," she recalled the Bible's words. "Ye devour widows' houses and for a pretence make long prayer. Woe unto you, scribes and Pharisees, hypocrites!"

Her office door opened and the orderly wheeled Rachel's chair inside. He told Rachel he would be back in an hour and quietly closed the door.

Pearl got up from her chair and walked over to Rachel's wheelchair, parking it beside her desk after shoving the other chair aside. She took Rachel's hand gently and said, "Good afternoon, Rachel. It is very nice to see you again."

In their last session, Rachel had begun to speak. The eyes that looked out of Rachel's pale face had begun to show emotion, though for now, only fear. As Pearl knew, fear was a useful emotion; more desirable than the void she had been gazing into before.

"Do you remember me?" Pearl asked, sitting down in her chair and leaning back. "I'm Pearl. We work together every other day. Have you had a chance to look outside? It's September now and you've been here for two months."

Pearl smiled a welcoming smile at Rachel and asked her if she could see the trees outside. Rachel started to turn her head toward the window but jerked it back and focused on Pearl's face.

"I like it when you look at me," Pearl said. "Today I thought you might like to look at the beautiful trees across the fields there. I think we're ready for a sharp frost and maybe tomorrow when you wake up those trees will have turned yellow, gold and red."

Pearl leaned forward, looked into Rachel's eyes and pointed to her own red satin blouse. "Can you tell me what color my blouse is, Rachel?"

"Red," Rachel said. To an inexperienced therapist, the voice would have been shocking. It sounded like a small child, perhaps three years old. "Red," Rachel repeated. "I like red."

"I know," Pearl agreed. "Your mother told me you liked red. She said you had a favorite doll with a red dress with white polka dots that you took everywhere with you. Do you remember that doll?"

"Dolly name Matilda," Rachel said.

"That's what your mother said."

"Dolly name Matilda." Rachel's eyes softened and began to change from fear to trepidation. Pearl knew the difference. Given her opinion that Rachel was not mentally ill, only shocked and perhaps emotionally damaged, she watched her eyes for every message. This was encouraging.

"During our last visit, you told me about your mother," Pearl said. "You said she played nice music and you liked to listen to her play."

"This little light of mine," Rachel sang softly in a cracked and high-pitched voice. She sounded like a child recovering from laryngitis. Mostly it was the sound of an unused voice, constricted by fear.

"I'm going to let it shine," Pearl sang back.

"This little light of mine," Rachel repeated, completely off key.

"I'm going to let it shine, let it shine, let it shine, let it shine," Pearl finished. "I love that song."

"Won't let Satan blow it out," Rachel sang.

"I'm going to let it shine," Pearl sang.

For the next ten minutes, Rachel and Pearl sang to each other, all the verses, over and over. Pearl felt like she was watching a miracle as Rachel's childlike face began to ease its painful expression and an inner light began to flicker. Faint as it was, the light was there and Pearl could see it. A sense of eagerness rose in Pearl's body. She'd felt this many times before. Hope! That's what it was. Hope! That wave of joy that threatened to envelop her when a patient had a breakthrough, when progress was made that surprised Pearl and reminded her why she worked with damaged minds. Hope!

When Pearl finished the last phrase of the song and leaned back in her chair, Rachel allowed her mouth to curve in a very slight smile as she drew her hands together and folded them in her lap.

"I like that song," Rachel said.

"I like it too." Pearl let a few moments pass. "Tell me what else you like."

Rachel hesitated. Fear returned to her eyes, but she never removed her gaze from Pearl's black moon face. It had become an anchor during their sessions.

"I like candy," Rachel said.

"Would you like a piece of candy now?" Pearl asked. She always kept a package of hard butterscotch candies in a lower drawer. Funny how often it had helped. "Have one of these," she said, offering a yellow cellophane-wrapped morsel to Rachel.

Rachel didn't lift her hand to accept the candy. She stared at it in silence.

Pearl held her hand closer. "Go ahead. It's delicious."

Rachel didn't move.

"Is there a reason you can't have the candy?"

"Daddy says I can't have any candy."

"Do you always obey your daddy?"

"Yes."

"Where is your daddy now? Perhaps we could ask him if it would be okay to have the candy this time."

"He won't say yes."

"What does your daddy say?"

"He tells me that he loves me, like in the song." She began singing, "Jesus loves me; this I know."

"For the Bible tells me so," Pearl sang.

"I don't remember the rest," Rachel said, beginning to speak with more ease. "But I know the song about the boat."

"Noah's boat?" Pearl asked as she dropped the candy back into the drawer.

"No, the 'Rock, Rock, Rock Little Boat' song." Rachel extended her hands beyond her knees and laced her fingers together. "Like this." She waited for Pearl to join her. "See, rock like this," Rachel directed Pearl. Pearl could hardly breathe as she slid her chair back from her desk so she could copy Rachel's motions. In a voice that gained strength with every word and matured in speech with each phrase, Rachel sang to Pearl. "Rock, rock, rock, little boat on the sparkling sea. Rock, rock, rock. King Jesus rides in thee."

Pearl's joy nearly burst her gold-toned buttons off her red blouse. Though Pearl possessed a beautiful, deep and rich alto voice and had grown up singing in her parents' church choir, she sat in her chair and sang along tonelessly with Rachel, learning the words but not the tune because Rachel wasn't able to reproduce it.

"Do you like boats?" Pearl asked, repositioning her chair closer to her desk. "I rode on a river boat once when I was a child. It had a big paddle wheel and lots of cheerful music."

"I don't know," Rachel said. "I like music."

So it is, thought Pearl. The key to this woman's fragile mind is music, the language of love, the language of the universe.

CHAPTER 16

The Forest for the Trees

"Thanks for giving up your day off," Joe said to Enoch as Enoch settled himself in Joe's dusty Pontiac. "Want a cup of coffee on the way?"

"All set," Enoch said. "Tell me what's eating at you."

Joe glanced over at Enoch as they exited Fenwell and headed east toward US Route 1. "I've got a bug up my butt, you might say. As you know, the Vogel case has gone to the DA; I couldn't hold it up any longer. Dead men don't talk; our key witness is incommunicado, and I think Jessie's lying through her teeth."

"What do you care?" Enoch asked. "Your job is done. You've done everything you could possibly do. It's not your family. What's your angle today?"

"Honestly, I don't know," Joe said. "A long shot at best." He repositioned his grip on the steering wheel and stared straight ahead. "What if…" He glanced at Enoch and back at the road. "What if I could find proof that Butch really did beat Rachel? What if someone could verify that wife beating ran in the family? Right now Jessie is in deep shit, deeper than she knows. She's trying to convince her own lawyer that Butch abused Rachel based on her gut feeling. Her lawyer's disclosure requests have included all records pertaining to complaints filed regarding Butch Vogel. There's nothing. Jessie's defense is looking weaker every day. Rachel's therapist doesn't believe Rachel will ever recall the incident and so far, Rachel has offered no information pertaining

131

to her marriage or Butch. So, I'm grabbing for straws. I'm trying to find Butch's father."

"Butch's father?" Enoch said. "I thought Butch had nothing to do with his father."

"How'd he get that Bible?" Joe asked.

"Good question."

"I've tracked his father down to a trailer park; trail's about a year old. He's kited some checks in the past and been arrested for disorderly conduct. He's a drunk and a bum. His last known address is at the far end of one of those parks on US Route 1. You know them, split by the widening of the highway years ago, and grandfathered in."

"Yeah. They look like a throwback to the forties."

"I think most of them house Gypsies and other transients. Sort of like a wart on a lovely ass," Joe offered.

"Peabody? A lovely ass?" Enoch laughed.

"One of these days, Peabody will declare them a health hazard and rip them out."

"Not in our lifetime."

"How are your parents holding up?" Joe asked. He drove up the sharply curved ramp to Route 1 North. "Reduced radius curves," he grumbled. "State's full of them."

"Okay," Enoch said. He looked over at Joe. "It's hard to tell."

"Jessie says your mother is falling apart."

"When did you see Jessie?"

"Last night."

"What's going on with you two? Since when did the lead detective have open season on the accused?"

"I care about her, you dolt," Joe said. He looked over at Enoch and grinned. "She said you wouldn't suspect it. She said for all your devotion to humanity, you weren't that keen on subtleties in your own family." Joe grinned as he passed a car going north. "But she thinks you're a saint. That's quite a responsibility."

"I wouldn't say the same of her," Enoch said. "The saint part."

"She said the misery quotient at home is higher than ever. Wondered how you could live there."

"How would she know? She's never there. She doesn't live there. She hardly ever comes to visit. She drops by on a Sabbath afternoon to feign the attentive daughter, gets into a spat with Father, pats her mother on the shoulder, and blows out pretending she's late for an important engagement." Enoch thought for a moment. "Fact is, I admire her to no ends. She's got a zest for life and a fascination with people that I envy."

"She's got spunk and brains," Joe said. "Though I think she's overestimated her abilities in this one. I still don't believe her story."

"I don't think she's lying," Enoch said. "Why should she risk prison for a sister she wasn't even close to? Jessie's not the bleeding heart type. If I were to list her shortcomings, I'd say Jessie's selfish and inconsiderate. I know that sounds unkind, but I can't imagine her doing anything self-sacrificing for anyone, least of all her family. If anything, Jessie's family has been a burden she's tried to unload since she was old enough to roller skate down the sidewalk. She treats family like a mosquito you brush away before it sucks your blood."

Enoch looked over at Joe. "Sorry, Joe, but Rachel is the one who believed that family was important and that you held it together no matter what. At least that's what I thought. That's why I can see Jessie conking Butch on the head with a pot but never Rachel. I think Rachel would have let Butch kill her before she'd have fought back."

Joe slowed the car and pulled toward the right shoulder of the highway. He entered the *Park Avenue* trailer park, his tires crunching over the gravel road that ran between the staggered rows of mobile homes. "I doubt these trailers ever saw the back end of a car," Joe said. "They all look like they were hauled here from the factory, plunked down on a frame of concrete blocks and left to die."

"Seedy," Enoch agreed rolling down his window to study the tiny bare yards and flapping canvas awnings. He turned to Joe. "Notice? No kids."

The gravel road ended in a T. Joe took a left and pulled up in front of a derelict trailer at the far end. The door of the trailer flapped back and forth on its squeaky aluminum hinges. Remnants of washday still clung to the drooping clothesline strung between a hook on the trailer and the branch of a dead tree. Newspapers blew about the hard-packed dirt yard and dead soldiers lay scattered around the cement block steps.

"Anyone home?" Joe yelled, as he stood perched on the top step and banged on the side of the trailer. He turned back to the car and motioned for Enoch to follow.

As they entered the dark trailer, Enoch asked, "Exactly what are we looking for?"

"Not sure," Joe said. "Just didn't think I should have all the fun."

They passed through the tiny kitchen where the smell of fermented garbage assailed their noses. Farther on they found nothing except a rotted cat in a back bedroom that looked like it had been strangled with a cheap sequined lady's belt.

"Looks like Fifi didn't make it," Joe said, holding his nose and backing out of the narrow room.

"Probably a blessing," Enoch said.

Joe threw Enoch a scoffing grin. "Jessie's right about you. What in hell ever made you turn cop after being a minister?"

Enoch laughed and jumped down from the trailer. "I was called."

"This was a waste of time," Joe said. "Sorry. Let's go see Jessie."

"What are you trying to do?" Enoch exclaimed as they got back into the car. "Contaminate the case?"

Joe looked closely at Enoch then stuck his head out his window and backed the car around carefully. He slowly retraced his path, stopped at the park exit, then eased into the traffic on Route 1.

"Nice to know a cop with a keen sense of right and wrong," Joe said to Enoch. "No, I'm not trying to damage the case. I love the girl. I'm not letting her go to prison."

Enoch stared at Joe. "Does she know that?"

"What? The love part or the prison part?"

"Both."

"If you want to know if I've declared my love? No. She makes it difficult to see her. Her lawyer will kill her if he finds out. As for prison, it will be over my dead body."

"A rather bold statement, don't you think?" Enoch said. "But I'm glad to hear it. If she's trying to take the blame for a murder that Rachel committed, she's playing a very foolish game. She keeps saying the charges are going to be dropped. Any chance of that?"

"Not so far."

"Well, I hope you know what you're doing," Enoch said, settling into his seat. "I don't think she's an easy one to handle; she's got quite an independent streak."

"Don't I know."

After a few minutes of contemplation Enoch asked, "Don't you think you're biting off more that you can chew? I mean; Jessie under indictment and her sister in a mental institution. Now that you mention it, if I think about it, things at home are not good at all. Not the best family to contemplate joining."

"Okay if we meet Jessie for lunch?" Joe interrupted. "There's a little seafood joint on the water in Beverly she suggested."

"You are the sly one," Enoch said. "Fine with me. The more I see of her, the more I like her. You know, I didn't know much about her when she was little, me being nine years older." He thought for a moment and asked, "Isn't she a bit young for you?"

Joe laughed.

***

Jessie greeted Enoch with a quick hug and smiled coolly at Joe. They found a table hidden behind a transparent plastic windscreen, obviously installed to extend the outdoor dining season on the weathered restaurant deck.

"Iced tea," Jessie said to the skinny boy in torn jeans. "What do you guys want?" They placed their orders for beverages and lobster rolls. "Best lobster rolls north of Boston," Jessie added. "I could live on them." She gazed across Beverly harbor, noting the dearth of boats now that summer was over. "I actually think the harbor is more beautiful without all the boats cluttering up the scene. Can you see that lighthouse way out on the point? I went there once to cover a story."

"Still getting the leftovers at work?" Enoch asked. He hadn't talked with Jessie for at least two weeks. They'd never been close and her visits at home were awkward.

"Work sucks," Jessie said. She flashed a thin smile at Joe. "There's no small amount of *schadenfreude* flowing around my desk. I sit there editing copy, rewriting shit stories and listening to the police scanner, while reporters, half as talented as I, get the breaking news, the big stories. I feel like a school kid assigned to sit in the corner every day."

"Probably good for your soul," Enoch said with a chuckle. "What is it they say about chastisement?"

"Was that meant as insight to life's experiences or as a lecture for my wayward ways?"

Enoch reached across the table and took her hand. "It was meant kindly. I'm worried about you. Guess I'm not the only one." Enoch looked at Joe and gave him a sly grin.

"Well frankly, I didn't think I'd be joining the ranks of poor schlumps facing a trial, for saving my sister's life." She glared openly at Joe and continued her complaint. "You know goddamn well Joe, that this thing has gone too far. I'm beginning to think Lady Justice not only is blind, but stupid to boot." She turned toward Enoch. "Sorry for snapping at you, but I'm beginning to lose my faith in the legal process. I've hired the best legal brain in town. He was supposed to get the charges dropped months ago. I'm paying through the nose for nothing."

Each man sat quietly eating his lobster roll. Seagulls swooped low, their bleating cries harsh on the ear. Enoch tossed a scrap of bread toward the edge of the dock. Six gulls swooped in for the kill.

"Don't do that," Jessie snapped. "They're flying rats."

In a less exasperated tone Jessie said to Enoch, "Living at home these days must be more difficult than ever. Does Mother ever stop crying?"

"Why ask me? I understand from Joe, you don't think I'm very observant." Jessie frowned at Joe, but let it pass. "And I think you're right. So I've tried thinking over things since July, you know, re-seeing things in my mind's eye. Perhaps I am a dolt." Enoch looked at Joe and grinned. "I always thought Pollyannas were female. I guess I wanted to see the best in people, especially my family."

Enoch put his half-eaten sandwich down and leaned forward, propping his elbows on the splintery picnic table. "Rachel was always a quiet little bird, pretty as a picture, and good as gold. I remember after she turned three or so, Father took her with him everywhere he went. In truth, I was a little jealous he never asked me." Enoch shrugged his shoulder. "But Mother always seemed to need me more than he did. Anyway, I remember that Rachel was always quiet, becoming more timid perhaps, and now that I think of it, back then, maybe a little withdrawn." He took his elbows off the table and sat back. "She was such a little trooper, getting that thyroid disease, and soldiering through, even when she became so hard to look at, that I honestly didn't give her a moment's notice. I went about my own pursuits, probably rather selfishly then. I was in school and little boys avoid their sisters anyway."

"Didn't the forced quiet in the house bother you?" Jessie asked.

"It had always been quiet," Enoch said. "I didn't think much about it because it was a way of life. You know how we were admonished to be circumspect and sober because a church member could be walking up the front steps at any moment? Mother trembled if there was any yelling or horseplay, as she called it. Of course, you were the fly in the ointment." Enoch grinned at Jessie. "When you came along, all hell broke loose; you were irrepressible."

"Enoch!" Jessie said. "You speak about it as though it was a slight irritant. Didn't you hate having to be so quiet? All you ever heard in that house was silence or Mother practicing her piano, or the muffled sounds of some atrocious student taking a lesson. For god's sakes, we couldn't play!"

"I don't remember not being able to play."

"Perhaps that's because every spare moment you had, Father had you in the basement helping him build those crappy birdhouses. That's not play, Enoch. That's work."

"Father raised a good bit of spare change with those birdhouses; that's how I got my bike. I felt like I was helping."

"I believe you, Enoch. But I wanted to play. I wanted to whoop it up." Jessie leaned closer to Enoch and looked him squarely in the eye. "Do you know how hard it is to play cowboys and Indians with no cowboys and tape over your mouth?" She grinned and leaned back. "My lips still hurt."

"I never played cowboys and Indians," Enoch said in a serious tone. Then he burst out laughing. "Remember? Father forbid us to have toy pistols because he didn't believe in guns? He must hate my current profession."

"I'm sure he does."

"On a more serious note, Jessie. Now that you have triggered my observation skills, I think Mother is suffering, more than we know."

"And the painfully obvious clues are, Sherlock?" Jessie asked.

"Father has forbidden her to talk to that therapist, Pearl."

"That's it!" Jessie slammed her hand on the rough surface of the picnic table. "I'll probably have fifty splinters," she mumbled as she scanned her hand and quieted her emotions. "I've avoided getting into our family issues all my life—"

"Uh, you call jumping into a fight between your sister and her husband avoiding family issues?" Enoch gave her a scoffing laugh.

Jessie flashed him a withering glare and continued. "What I was trying to say is that I stay out of family issues because I have a conviction about bad marriages: both people usually deserve each other. Though after watching Rachel and Butch, I'm beginning to think, the blame isn't always equal."

"Let me assure you it's not," Enoch said, glancing over at Joe.

"I live and work in Boston. I can't drive up to Fenwell on a whim, especially now that my butt is nailed to my chair. But you can do something about this."

"I took her once and Father got pretty huffy about it," Enoch said. "Then he apologized to me privately and I thought things were okay."

"You would." She sat back and looked at Enoch more kindly. "Either you drive Mother to meet with that therapist, or you stand up to Father and make sure Mother has her freedom. Trying to restrict her to that sepulcher of a house is mental and emotional abuse. You have to stop it! Besides, what is he afraid of? He should be glad. He was always telling her she was going over the edge, you know, undermining her self-confidence, playing the despot, keeping her in her subservient position."

Jessie turned her attention to Joe who had sat quietly listening to the two siblings hash out their family issues. "I'm sure it's because of Father that I made up my mind that no man would ever, and I mean, never, pull that shit with me. Maybe that's what has bothered me so much about poor Rachel. Butch was a younger version of our father. Maybe that's why Rachel married him. Rachel never stood up to Father and I'm positive she never stood up to Butch."

Jessie looked off to the horizon then said to Enoch, "Anyway, if

Father were a decent husband, he should be glad she has someone she wants to talk to. He should welcome the opportunity for her, be supportive."

"I'm seeing the opposite," Enoch said. "It does surprise me."

"That's because you never paid attention," Jessie reminded him. "Mother worshiped you and Father had no complaints about you. What more could he ask for than a son who was a little saint and grew up to be a minister? You were truly a gift."

"That's enough," Enoch said. His tone was kind, just firm enough to deliver the message that he didn't like life on a pedestal and never had.

"Okay," Jessie said. "I'm sorry. Look, you work things out at home for Mother to have the freedom she needs to meet with Rachel's therapist. I'll call Mother while Father is at work and encourage her to go."

"Don't overwhelm her with your concern," Enoch said with a friendly smile. "We don't want her going into shock."

Jessie threw a crumpled napkin at Enoch's head and said, "I'm done. Let's go."

CHAPTER 17

Singing for Sanity

Pearl always arrived at work an hour early. It gave her time to preview her day, make sure all required files had been brought to her office, call the records department if any were missing, and simply compose herself from her commute. She didn't mind driving but as traffic increased on Route 128, tempers and bad driving habits seemed to increase proportionately.

She glanced at the newspaper headlines: another road rage incident. This isn't going to get any better, she thought, as she sipped her first cup of coffee. She flipped quickly through the pages of the Boston Beacon, a rag she read quickly and superficially. Truth was, Pearl hated reading newspapers. Best way in the world to get depressed, she always told her husband. Shut down the media and the whole world would improve.

Against her better judgment, Pearl found herself combing the papers for news of the Vogel murder. It was rare for her to have any connection to an ongoing murder case and she found her curiosity to ferret out every little snippet of news far exceeded her good judgment in avoiding negative stories. She'd even picked up a few issues of the Shyler Clarion, a typical small town paper that trumpeted the murder on the front page, even when nothing newsworthy came to light. "Thank god," she breathed to herself as she tossed the papers into her wastebasket, for the privilege that covered therapist and patient communications. Hers was one profession that was shielded from pestering reporters.

Her phone rang, jolting her out of her mental ruminations. "I hope it's not that damned attorney again," she said out loud. "Never saw the likes for his efforts to ignore the law, an attorney, of all people. He should know."

She picked up the phone, spoke briefly, then hung it up. "Speaking of reporters, the Lord works in mysterious ways." She continued mumbling to herself as she pulled Rachel's file from her pile, made a note, and returned it to her afternoon stack. "That Jessie may be a murderer, but she's a good sister."

***

Pearl had run an errand during her lunch hour and was hustling as quickly as her large body burdened by six months of pregnancy would allow. Driven by a premature hard frost, early winter winds bit through her fall jacket. She struggled with each step up the main staircase to the third floor where her office was located. At this point in the building, the balustrades were free of the wire caging that lined every set of stairs in the wards. Usually thoughts of the wire caging and the locked doors and the bars on the windows depressed her. But today, she couldn't stop the musical tape that ran in an endless loop in her brain.

She hurried into her office, locked her purse in a lower drawer of her desk, and slipped the key into her pocket. The musical phrases of "Amazing Grace" continued their repetitive process in her head as an orderly knocked on her door and pushed it open.

Pearl rose from her desk and started for the door to greet her patient. She stopped short. Standing in the doorway, just in front of the orderly, was Rachel. As though Rachel had always walked to her sessions, Pearl approached Rachel and extended her hand to guide Rachel to the chair next to her desk. Pearl was dying to ask the orderly what had precipitated Rachel's choice to walk today, but she bit her tongue, said a pleasant good-bye to the orderly, and took her seat behind her desk.

Pearl quickly skimmed through the ward supervisor's most recent report to see if the change from wheelchair to walking had been noted. Nothing. She flipped through her notes from Rachel's last session buying time to get a better grip on her emotions. My lord, she said to herself. She loves music. She's beginning to talk, and today she's walked right in here, bold as brass. Clasping her hands together at her breasts, Pearl rolled her large eyes toward the ceiling, breathed a soft prayer of gratitude, and turned toward Rachel, her black eyes wide with warmth and expectation.

Rachel met Pearl's steady gaze. Pearl opened her mouth and began singing "Amazing Grace" in her rich alto voice. Rachel kept her eyes locked onto Pearl's face and slowly, in that cracked, immature voice of a sick child, began to sing along with Pearl.

For the next ten minutes, Pearl and Rachel sang. Pearl thought her heart would truly burst with joy at Rachel's improvement. As Pearl sang, Rachel's face began to shine with her passion for the song. A light, extinguished long ago, flickered to life in Rachel's eyes as she dared to peek out from behind the wall of fear.

Inspired more by instinct than formal training, Pearl leaned across the corner of her desk and took Rachel's pale and trembling hand into her large black hand. Rachel looked down at her hand that had disappeared into Pearl's, then up at Pearl's broad face, and smiled.

"Lord God," Pearl breathed to herself. *Lord God, Lord God.* How we humans hunger for love, for a touch, for the warmth of one small gesture.

Still holding Rachel's hand, Pearl said, "So you love to sing?" Pearl released Rachel's hand and sat back in her chair. It creaked under her weight. "What else do you love? Since you sing like a bird, do you like birds?"

A cloud of apprehension passed over Rachel's face. Her expression turned to confusion, then settled back into fear.

"Daddy loves birds," Rachel said. "I don't like them. We watch them together, but I'm afraid."

Scared of moving too quickly but sensing the peeling away of a

143

thick layer, Pearl plunged ahead, choosing her words carefully and maintaining her warm smile on which Rachel's gaze locked like a beacon.

"What else do you and Daddy do?"

"Daddy helps me," Rachel said, her face reflecting a little more comfort.

"How does Daddy help you?" Pearl asked. Her voice was encouraging but gentle.

"Daddy helps me be clean."

"Clean?" Pearl asked. "Does he bathe you or wash your hair?"

"No. He helps me be clean."

"What do you mean, helps you be clean? Does he put soap on your hands and run water over them and dry them on a towel?"

"No." Rachel grew impatient with Pearl's lack of comprehension.

"He makes me clean for Jesus, you know, like this." Rachel stuck out her tongue as far as she could and made lapping motions.

A chill gripped Pearl's racing heart. The excitement that had been threatening to overwhelm her with hope, evaporated, leaving her feeling icy cold. She felt like she'd stepped into an ancient burial vault. Her words came out in suppressed bursts.

"Where does he lick you?" Pearl asked. A heightened anxiety at an awful truth pushed her heart rate into the red zone.

"I can't tell you that," Rachel said. She closed her eyes.

"Why can't you tell me?" Pearl asked.

"Because he made me promise."

Pearl pressed her hand swiftly to her chest as her gorge threatened to rise and cause her to vomit. She took deep breaths, knowing full well the months of morning sickness were long past. This feeling of nausea was caused by revulsion at what her instincts were telling her and what her logical mind was refusing to accept. Rachel still had her eyes closed.

Pearl looked out her windows at the distant woods, the trees now a smoky haze of bare limbs and twigs without their brilliant autumnal colors. Oh give me grace, she prayed silently. Give me the grace to accept the truth and help heal this poor child. Yes, she said inside her head. I know these things happen. Yes, I should be fully prepared for hearing these revelations. They do not surprise me. But I seem doomed to fight reality with each new tragedy. I so want it not to be true this time. I wish it hurt me less, but it never does.

Drawing on her deep reservoir of faith in human nature at the same time it was under assault, Pearl began to sing "Amazing Grace" softly. She sat very still and watched Rachel's drawn face; faded from lack of sunshine, and whitened by her own slow inner dying. After a few agonizing moments, traces of color crept back into Rachel's cheeks. She opened her eyes and looked at Pearl. She smiled faintly and began to sing with Pearl. "I once was lost, but now am found, was blind, but now, I see."

Fearing the unknown—despite all the books, theses and research, Pearl believed the mind was an unknown—Pearl picked up the phone and called for the orderly to escort Rachel back to her ward. Ending the session early was the safest thing for Pearl. She needed time to digest this information. Plus, her early morning phone call that had brought encouragement now weighed heavily. She needed time to think now that Willa would be arriving in thirty minutes. How resilient was Willa and would she be able to shed any new light on the relationship between her husband and her elder daughter?

CHAPTER 18

Suffer Little Children

Pearl resumed singing with Rachel until the orderly arrived. With a reassuring pat on Rachel's shoulder, Pearl watched her leave, then rushed to the bathroom to wash her face and regain her composure. The next session might be brutal.

Enoch entered Pearl's office with his mother. It was obvious he'd taken time off during his duty day to assist his mother with her mission.

He greeted Pearl and saw his mother to the chair beside Pearl's desk. "You call me when you're done, Mother," Enoch said, switching his uniform cap to place it under his other arm. "I'll drive you home." He turned toward the door, and then turned back. Bending close to his mother's ear he whispered, "And don't you worry about Father. I'll be home tonight for supper; I promise."

Pearl beamed her all-embracing smile on Willa who made a feeble attempt to return a smile, but failed.

Hoping that Willa's trembling would lessen if she proceeded slowly, Pearl said, "Rachel loves music. I trust she got that from you."

"I do love music," Willa said, her eyes searching Pearl's face for approval. "It is my passion."

"Mine too," Pearl said, "though I don't have much time to indulge it nowadays. I miss church most Sundays." She smiled ruefully and added, "My mother would not be happy with me."

"Was your mother religious?" Willa asked. She appeared to be relieved the conversation wasn't going to focus on her.

"My mother followed religion, and gave her heart to God," Pearl said. "But unlike so many religious people who profess but don't practice, my mother lived her beliefs."

"Did you love her?" Willa asked. Pearl smiled to herself. Who was interviewing whom?

"I loved her," Pearl said. "Is your mother still living?" Time to turn the tables.

"I never knew her," Willa said.

"I thought both your parents and Floyd's were alive when you two were married."

"No," Willa said. She explained the death of her biological parents and the adoption by her aunt and uncle.

"So you grew up calling your aunt, Mother?" Pearl asked.

"She insisted."

Pearl sensed this topic could wait for another time, so she picked up from their prior session.

"By the time you had Jessie, you and Floyd had moved to Buffalo, New York. Is that what you told me?"

"Yes. Floyd received his first posting as pastor of his own congregation. There was a good-sized church and a church school, grades one through ten. Though he didn't teach, the school was his responsibility. He was never happier."

"Was there anything specific that contributed to Floyd's happiness?"

Willa looked puzzled.

"Perhaps the question doesn't matter."

Willa relaxed. "What I say rarely matters," she said glancing away to the windows and the bleak autumn scene outside. "Floyd rarely asks me questions. Even when he does, he doesn't listen to my answers." She shrugged her shoulders in defeat and looked back at Pearl. "It doesn't matter much."

"Willa?" Pearl began. Concern was pecking away inside her head. With Floyd appointed guardian to Rachel, she'd become anxious about Rachel's future, and was now terrified about

147

Rachel's past. Trusting that Willa was stronger than she appeared, Pearl plunged down the path of discovery she felt compelled to travel.

"Do you believe that Floyd loves your children?"

"Oh, yes!" Willa exclaimed, her eyes opening wide with surprise. "We both love our children, very much, no matter what they've done."

"Did Floyd help you with the children when they were little, when they needed baths and feeding? Did he share that work with you?"

"No. Floyd never fed the children or bathed and dressed them. He's a minister. Caring for the house and the children was my job."

"Did he spend time with the children?"

"Yes. We always spent time with them. All good parents make sure they spend time with their children."

"Were there any special activities that your husband shared with any of the children, like playing ball, sports, skiing?"

"We don't believe in paying homage to competitive sports, you know, the professional teams. Floyd didn't like baseball anyway. Of course, we couldn't afford to go skiing. Neither Floyd nor I learned to ski. That's for rich people."

"So what did you do for recreation?"

"We read the Bible, listened to music, and attended church and religious events. On Sabbaths we had picnics, visited nature reserves and gave Bible lessons. Floyd always liked birds though. Sometimes he would go off to a local park to roam the meadows, communing with nature for inspiration for his sermons."

"Did he go alone?" Pearl asked.

"Not always. Sometimes he took Rachel. He said she was so quiet and well-behaved he hardly knew she was there."

"How old was she when he took her to the park?"

"It was after we moved to Buffalo. She was three or so. She adored him. If he told her to be quiet, she was quiet as a mouse.

She loved to be with him." Willa seemed to travel back in her mind, recalling things, sifting through memories and selecting those she wished to share.

"I remember when little Rachel was four or so, and Enoch was in school, I could go over to the church and practice the organ for hours without worrying about Rachel. When I would return, she'd be sitting right there in Floyd's study, quiet as a mouse, coloring in her pretty Bible coloring book or playing with her rubber drink-and-piddle dolly."

Willa shifted in her chair and said, "Now Jessie. Jessie was another story. Never played with dolls. She was always making noise, disrupting everything, whooping like a wild Indian, racing through the house. There were times I had to tape her mouth shut so Floyd could concentrate in his study." Willa paused and looked furtively at Pearl. "Wouldn't you know it would be Jessie who would kill someone? She always flaunted religion and ignored its teachings. Floyd warned me when she went off to live in Boston that she would come to an evil end."

"Do you believe in evil?" Pearl asked.

"Yes, I do," Willa answered with asperity. "I believe the Devil is busy doing his work all around the world, twenty-four hours a day."

"Do you believe that good people can do evil things?"

Willa opened her mouth to answer; then stopped herself. Fear flitted in her pale green eyes.

Ouch, thought Pearl. Hit too close to the bone there.

The spunk that Willa had shown when speaking of the Devil evaporated as she gave consideration to the question. She made a futile reach for a tissue but drew her hand back empty. "What do you mean?"

"I mean, do you know of any evil things in Rachel's past that could contribute to her present condition? Anything that could have hurt her, frightened her, shocked her?"

"I took the best care of her I could," Willa said, her voice reverting to its old whining tone. "I cannot be blamed for anything anyone else might have done. I was a good mother." Tears welled up in Willa's eyes and trickled down her putty-like cheeks. Willa's skin looked unhealthy and undernourished, though Willa was clearly overweight. Willa's cheeks looked like if you poked them, the dent would remain, like a severe case of edema.

"Willa," Pearl said gently as she pushed the box of tissues closer to her. "I believe you were a good mother. I truly do. I have a question to ask you. I know you came here out of great courage, and I believe great need. I believe some of that need is for yourself, and some of it is for Rachel." Pearl waited while Willa grabbed a fistful of tissues, wiped her eyes and blew her nose.

"Is it possible that Floyd behaved toward Rachel in a manner that was not fatherly, and that you know about it?"

Willa let out a tiny scream, covered her face with her tissue-filled hands, and burst into a paroxysm of sobs. Pearl waited while Willa wept. No wonder the woman needed to come. How does a person carry this kind of grief and guilt and stay healthy and normal? They don't.

When Willa had calmed to quiet weeping, Pearl tried again.

"I fear what I have to ask, Willa, but time is important. I need your help. Together we need to help Rachel. May I go ahead?"

Willa sniffed but made an obvious and apparently genuine effort to buck up and compose her frazzled emotions.

"When a patient regresses to a place of silence, then slowly emerges, moving through the early years of childhood, and hopefully returning to the present, it tells us something." She looked at Willa's troubled face but saw a spark of determination burning in her teary eyes. "I won't trouble you with a lengthy explanation. What I will tell you is that from my experience, and I believe this is applicable to Rachel, a shock, or multiple shocks can push the person into a need for escape. The forms their escapes take are varied. Some become hostile, hurting those around them or themselves. Some become substance abusers:

drug addicts and alcoholics. And some withdraw emotionally and become totally unreachable. In Rachel's case, I think she has tried to escape by closing herself down, attempting to put a protective barrier between herself and the world."

Willa stopped sniffling, wiped her nose again and listened intently.

"We don't know what Rachel saw the night her husband died. I'm not sure we ever will. But, during the last few sessions, Rachel has given me much encouragement in her ability to recover."

Willa began weeping again; this time in obvious relief.

"Willa," Pearl continued, leaning toward Willa and searching her face. "I believe something happened to Rachel, when she was three to four years old." Willa held her breath and clenched her fists but kept her eyes locked on Pearl.

"I think you can tell me what happened if I help you."

Pain and terror washed in alternate waves over the pathetic woman's face. Pearl could feel Willa's fingernails cutting into her own palms. Willa's shoulders began to shake but still she kept her eyes glued on Pearl. Her breathing became labored gasps.

"Rachel says her father helped keep her clean," Pearl began gently. Willa winced. "She made an exaggerated lapping motion with her tongue. Can you tell me what she was trying to say?" Willa stared at Pearl and didn't move a muscle. Her shoulders stopped shaking; she was slowly transposing herself into stone.

Pearl leaned back in her chair and turned her gaze toward the woods in an effort to break the tension. She took a few deep breaths and relaxed her shoulders. Better change course, she thought.

"Enoch told me about the story that Jessie wrote that caused Floyd to drive a young man out of the house and forced Rachel to undergo a physical examination."

"She'd been defiled," Willa said in a wooden tone.

"Did you prove that?" Pearl asked, leaning forward and speaking with extreme gentleness. "Didn't Rachel scream so badly and resist the physician's touch so violently that he never completed the examination? Wasn't she traumatized for weeks?"

Willa looked down at her fists and nodded her head in the affirmative.

"Do you know of any reason why a young girl, other than being frightened and angry, would react so violently to a doctor? Is it because she had been touched inappropriately in her genitals in the past and had formed phobic reactions? Is it because her father had abused her when she was little and couldn't defend herself? Did loving her father lock her into a secret world where bad things happened to good little girls and there was no way she would ever be good enough for any man, not even Jesus?"

Willa's stony physique crumbled. She burst into tears, crying out, "I told him to stop. When I found out, I went to him and screamed at him to stop. He said he'd have me locked up in a lunatic asylum for such insane accusations. He told me no one would believe me, that I was crazy and had a sick imagination. And then," Willa paused. She gulped great mouthfuls of air like she was having an asthma attack. "And then…"

Pearl reached over and took one of Willa's trembling hands. "And then?"

"He took me to bed and had sex with me, violent sex, brutal sex. He hurt me."

"How did he hurt you?"

With both fists pressing against her lower jaw, Willa closed her eyes and whispered. "After he'd satisfied himself, he grabbed my left breast and twisted it." She stopped to quell the tremor in her voice. "He twisted my breast until I screamed. Then he twisted it again. I thought he would tear it off." She stopped speaking and opened her eyes.

Pearl guessed that Willa was passing through some unknown valley of terror and could see a ray of safety somewhere in the distance, but she wasn't there yet.

Willa wiped the perspiration off her face, still gasping for air, and continued. "'If you ever tell another person of your deranged fantasies,' he said, 'I will rip your breast off your body. Do you hear me?'"

Pearl folded her fat arms across her huge breasts and looked at Willa, in a sense transferring her inner strength into the heart of this courageous woman, lending her life support while she struggled for air to breathe, the right to exist. Pearl knew that Willa's world, as she had known it all her adult life, had come crashing down. Her instincts told her that Willa had the inner strength to rebuild her world in a mold that would fit her much better. As they exchanged looks, Willa confirmed Pearl's belief.

After some minutes of silence, Willa's breathing slowed. She resettled her shoulders and raised her chin.

"May God forgive me for what I'm going to say, but, when Rachel got that thyroid disease, I thanked him. He made little Rachel so unappealing to Floyd that Floyd began to avoid her. He never took her anywhere with him again. He rarely went near her. He never touched her again that I could see." She looked at Pearl with pleading eyes. "I was grateful that God had made my little girl ugly to save her. How evil am I?"

"You're not evil, Willa," Pearl said. "You are a good Christian woman who has been given too much to bear. You are the kind of Christian who devotes her life to goodness and love but finds a world full of cruelty and hate."

"But Jesus teaches us to turn the other cheek." Willa's eyes had dropped to her twisting fingers. "Love those who despise us. That we are all born in sin and none of us is worthy of his love. That in order to find life everlasting, we must first lose our life in Jesus. Without his saving grace, we are nothing." She began wringing her restless hands. "I'm so ashamed of myself. I couldn't protect my daughter. I loved Floyd so much. I wanted him to love me. I wanted him to want me and hold me and ravish me. I was a despicable woman who caused him great suffering."

"Willa," Pearl said with a tone of authority in her voice. Willa looked up. "Willa?" Pearl stared at Willa and locked her again in her gaze. "You must never be ashamed of yourself again. You must never even think of being ashamed. Shame is the great weapon that abusers of religion use to control and cow weaker people. Shame teaches self-loathing. It convinces us we are unacceptable, unlovable and unworthy. When we feel unworthy, we can't protect others. We can't protect ourselves. We ask nothing for ourselves, not even good mental health."

Willa dropped her eyes to her lap again but leaned slightly forward as though she couldn't hear enough of Pearl's wisdom.

"I may be wrong," Pearl continued, "but I believe that both you and Rachel reflect religious teachings at their worst. Whatever God we believe in, never designed us to feel unworthy of being. No loving God, if he is a loving God, wants us to walk in shame, feeling unloved and unlovable." She paused and smiled at Willa as Willa raised her head. "My mother had that rare balance of piety and self-acceptance, a solid grasp of the role of religion versus common sense. There are times I wish my mother could have been mother to the world."

Willa responded to the remark with a faint smile. "We'd all be black," she said.

"And fat," Pearl added with good humor. "My mother understood the role that religion has played in the history of man. What she understood most clearly was that religion, whatever religion you embrace, must be taught with love and common sense. Religion without compassion is empty doctrine; like parenting without love. I believe you experienced that. Parenting without love casts a child adrift. Unhealthy teachings in the name of religion can destroy a child's self-esteem. Healthy self-esteem on the other hand forms the core of individual responsibility. We are all responsible for what we say and do. Good mental health begins at birth, not at the altar of any god. Good mental health is not dependent on religion or creed but on self-respect and good values."

When Willa had entered Pearl's office earlier that afternoon, her face had appeared crushed, like it had caved in on itself. As Pearl studied Willa's face now, she saw more openness, color in her cheeks, hope in her eyes. "That's what I believe," she said softly. "That's exactly what I believe."

Pearl shifted her position in her chair, grabbed a file in a most businesslike manner and snapped a pencil into her hand. "Willa, you are a strong woman. I need your help. Time is truly of the essence."

Willa looked surprised and puzzled.

"With your fine blood flowing through her veins, I believe Rachel is going to be okay. It will take time, but my hopes are high. What we need to do now, is form a circle of protection around Rachel and the first order of business is to remove Floyd from guardianship."

"Oh, no," Willa cried, fear threading its ugly self back into her voice. "He won't agree to that. He's her guardian. He has to look out for her; see to the maintenance of her home, collect the rents, and manage her money."

"Willa," Pearl said sternly but with compassion. "Floyd is not the person to stand guardian over Rachel. He has defaulted on his parental responsibilities at the most basic level. While I don't doubt Butch played his role in further harming Rachel, I believe her emotional problems began with her father."

Willa listened attentively.

"Would you consider putting Rachel's care and guardianship into Enoch's hands? I assess him to be a responsible and caring man."

"I don't know about Floyd," Willa said. Pearl could see the battle in Willa's thoughts as her eyes darted back and forth, searching for answers on the walls, the desk and back to Pearl's face.

"Would you trust Enoch with caring for you if you couldn't care for yourself?"

"Yes. Definitely," Willa said. "But I can't ask Floyd to relinquish his responsibilities to Enoch. He would be very angry at me."

"You won't have to ask, Willa." Pearl closed the file and stood up to stretch her bones. "Do you know two hours have flown by?" She smiled at Willa and motioned for her to stand and stretch.

"Floyd will never agree," Willa said as she rose stiffly from her chair. "I can't make him do that."

"All you have to do Willa is stay committed to your own health and to Rachel's. You will need to speak up for Rachel when the time comes. Can you do that?"

"What do you mean?" Willa looked up at the larger woman with concern.

"The courts will make the change in guardianship at my request. Floyd can fight and have his secrets exposed for public scrutiny, or, he can quietly acquiesce and hope his harmful actions stay within the family circle."

"Oh," Willa said in awe.

CHAPTER 19

A Time of Reckoning

It was October 5th, almost a week since her last visit with Pearl. Willa had been a bit more nervous than usual, wondering what would happen when Floyd was asked to relinquish his guardianship of Rachel. She hadn't breathed a word about the last session to a soul. Today she'd spent the afternoon making Floyd's favorite desert, apple pie. The air in the kitchen was heavy with its sweet cinnamony aroma.

"Hello," Willa said as Floyd entered their home wearing his most pleasant smile and giving Willa a little kiss on her cheek. His kiss was such a rare event that Willa was startled but she recovered quickly and offered to take his coat.

"Goodness, such a chill today," Willa said as she hurried to the closet near the front door. She took great care of Floyd's fine wool overcoat since it served him daily at the conference office and was also his Sabbath best. "The leaves were blowing in blustery circles across the driveway, like little hobgoblins rushing helter-skelter searching for candy," she said as she returned to the kitchen. Halloween was only three weeks away and she ached to purchase some bags of tiny candy bars to place in a plastic pumpkin on their front steps. But that would require defiance of Floyd's religious beliefs. After all, the origins of Halloween were pagan, not Christian.

"When will supper be ready?" Floyd asked as he flipped through the mail on the counter.

"The usual," Willa said as she opened the oven and stuck a chicken thigh with a fork. "It's still pink, but almost done."

Floyd appeared to be heading into the living room to read as was his custom while waiting for supper. Instead he stopped at the doorway to the dining room and in the most casual of voices said, "I got a phone call from Pearl Whitman late this afternoon. She wants Enoch to be Rachel's guardian. You know anything about that?"

Willa dropped the greasy fork on the floor and froze.

"Perhaps she knows you have too many responsibilities already," Willa said in a whispery thin voice.

Floyd leaned casually on the door jam. His eyes were intent but he retained his pleasant expression. "Did you tell her I had too many responsibilities?"

Willa bent to retrieve the fork and turned her back to Floyd, taking the fork to the sink and scrubbing it vigorously under the faucet. "No."

"Exactly what did you tell her?" Floyd asked. Slowly, he crossed the kitchen and approached Willa. Like a giant frog's tongue snatching a fly from the air, Floyd thrust out his arm, grabbed Willa and spun her around to face him. Water splashed in all directions. He leaned down into her face and said, "What exactly did you tell that black bitch to make her insist I withdraw as Rachel's guardian?"

"Nothing," Willa said, her voice quavering as she tried to turn back to the sink and turn off the faucet. She had heard this tone from Floyd before. It conjured memories of severe pain. "She asked questions. I offered nothing."

Floyd flung Willa around against the kitchen table, knocking the chairs askew and sliding most of the plates and silverware on the floor. The glasses crashed and shattered in smithereens.

"What did you tell her?" Floyd pressed her backward over the table. As the table skidded across the floor, Willa lost her footing and crumpled into a heap at Floyd's feet. With his highly polished brown leather dress shoe he delivered a perfectly centered blow between her legs.

Willa screamed and doubled over.

The back door flew open.

Still in uniform, minus his weapons, Enoch entered the kitchen braced for action. He glanced past his father and searched the space for the source of that bloodcurdling scream. Then he saw his mother crumpled in a heap on the floor at his father's feet. He grasped his father's arms and brought them to Floyd's back. At the same moment he reached to detach the handcuffs he wore on duty, but he had none.

Though two inches shorter than his father, Enoch whipped him aside, faced him away, and slammed him spread-eagle against the kitchen wall. "Don't move," Enoch said, his breath coming in short rasping gasps, not from exertion but from the realization of what was happening. "Let me help you up," Enoch said to Willa as he reached both hands beneath her armpits and lifted her to an upright position.

Enoch kicked chunks of broken glass aside and led his mother to a chair. As he tried to ease her down she screamed and insisted on standing up. "What in the name of god happened here?" Enoch asked, wrapping his arms around Willa to steady her while her body shook with uncontrollable sobs. "What happened?" Enoch looked down at his mother's disheveled face and spoke even more gently. "What did Father do to you?"

"I didn't do anything to her," Floyd said with disgust as he turned to face Enoch and grabbed a chair to sit down.

"Stay against that wall!" Enoch yelled.

"You can't talk to me like that," Floyd said, disregarding his son and sitting down in the chair. "I'm your father and this is my house."

"Can you sit down now?" Enoch asked Willa.

"It hurts," Willa sobbed into Enoch's dark blue uniform shirt.

"Where did he hit you?" Enoch asked, taking a step back to examine her injuries.

"He didn't hit me."

"What did he do?" Enoch's voice was rising. "What did he do to you?"

"He kicked me," Willa whimpered, returning to Enoch's arms, the only spot of safety in her home.

"Where?" Enoch demanded. "Show me where."

"I can't," Willa cried. Her anguished voice tore at Enoch's heart.

"I'll take you to the hospital," Enoch said.

"You will not," Floyd said. "She's making it all up. She fell."

Enoch stepped back from his mother again and saw the stream of blood running down the inside of her leg below the hem of her dress.

"You're going to the hospital," he said, turning off the faucet as he grabbed a fistful of clean towels from a nearby drawer. He shepherded his mother toward the back door and helped her into her coat. Before he opened the door he said to his father, "You can either stay here and wait for our return, or I'll have an officer pick you up and take you to the station; it's your choice."

***

While the doctor was examining Willa, Enoch put in a call to Jessie, tracking her down with her pager.

"What the hell happened?" Jessie demanded when she called him back on the pay phone in the emergency waiting room. "Why is Mother in the hospital?" After a brief and cryptic explanation from Enoch, Jessie said, "We can be at the hospital in thirty minutes."

"Probably better if you go to the house. I'll bring her home as soon as she's done."

Enoch hung up the phone. It took him a moment to realize Jessie had said, "We."

Then he put in an emergency call to Pearl Whitman.

Half an hour later, a nurse in a wrinkled uniform wheeled Willa out through the stainless steel doors, followed by a doctor in pale green scrubs.

"Are you okay, Mother?" Enoch asked rushing to greet her and leaning down to peer into her downcast eyes. She didn't raise her head nor did she look at him.

Gently the doctor pulled Enoch into a quiet corner behind a row of empty gurneys.

"She'll be okay in a few days," he said.

"What happened?" Enoch asked, his breath again coming in short gasps. This couldn't be happening to his family, not *his* mother, not *his* father.

"She received a severe blow to her genitals, lacerating the labia majora and the labia minora. It took quite a few stitches to put everything back in place." At the shock in Enoch's face, the doctor stopped speaking. "I'm sorry," he resumed. "I know this is your mother. I believe the pubic bone is bruised though it is not easy to detect at this time." The doctor scribbled his signature on a prescription and handed it to Enoch. "I don't know how this happened, but I trust you do. She needs rest and safety. She should wash herself daily with an iodine solution and take this prescription for pain. The physical damage should heal in a week or two, except perhaps for the bruising." The doctor turned away then halted and turned back to Enoch. "This is out of my area of expertise, but, I think the bruising is more than physical. Is there a possibility of her receiving attention for that?"

Enoch dropped his eyes in shame, then faced the doctor more openly. "Yes. There is. I will see to that."

***

When Enoch pulled into the driveway of his parents' home, Willa asked, "Who's here?" She had been silent on the ride home. Now her voice was filled with anxiety.

"Looks like Detective D'nardo's car," Enoch said.

"Are you arresting Floyd?" Willa lurched forward and stared

out of the windshield in terror. "This will destroy him! He will kill me!"

Enoch shut off the engine and went around the car to assist his mother. "He will never touch you again," Enoch assured her as he gently guided her into the house. "Never again."

The brightly lit kitchen was like a tableau. Someone had picked up the dishes and silverware and swept up the broken glass. Floyd sat at the far end of the table, rage emanating from his face reducing his pupils to black pinpoints.

Joe and Jessie were also at the table, sitting across from each other, neither speaking. The old wooden lazy Susan had been restored to the center of the table, but it was bare. The sugar bowl with the cracked lid and the cow-shaped creamer that had sat there since Willa had set up housekeeping with Floyd, were missing.

As Enoch and Willa entered the kitchen Floyd jumped up and rushed toward Enoch yelling, "What right do you have to call the police?" Joe pushed his chair back and stood. Floyd glanced at Joe and stopped a few steps from Enoch and Willa. "Nothing happened here. You said if I stayed here you wouldn't call the police." He cast a belligerent glance toward Jessie. "Why in the name of god did you bring Jessie into this? It's none of her business."

"Sit down, Father," Enoch said evenly, not looking Floyd in the eye.

Enoch tried to help his mother toward an empty chair at the end of the table opposite where Floyd had been sitting but she stood still, her eyes fixed on the lazy Susan. She cast a vacant look around the room and whimpered, "Where are my pretty dishes?"

Enoch eased Willa toward the chair and lowered her slowly, waiting while she absorbed the pain. "You'll be all right," he said softly into her ear. He went to the sink and filled a glass of water and offered it to his mother with the small bottle of pills he'd picked up at the drug store.

Floyd went back to his chair but remained standing, thrumming an angry rhythm on the back with his fingers. Past his head Enoch could read the framed sampler that his mother had embroidered when she was a child, *"God Bless our Happy Home."* Enoch turned his eyes away and exchanged grim glances with Joe and Jessie.

"Sit down, Father," Enoch repeated, heading into the dining room for a fifth chair. "We have some family business to attend to." Floyd sat down and leaned back, releasing his breath in an exhalation of exasperation and disgust.

Joe resumed his seat but kept his eyes on Floyd.

"I don't know what you think you're doing, Enoch," Floyd said when Enoch came back with the chair. "I'm the head of this house."

Enoch ignored his father's comment.

"What in the hell went on here?" Jessie asked, flashing an angry glare at her father and a curious look at her mother. To Enoch she said, "Father says mother fell and you raced her to the hospital like she'd fallen from a twenty-story building." Jessie reached over and gingerly took her mother's hand; it wasn't her practice to touch her mother voluntarily. She patted Willa's hand and asked, "Are you okay now?"

"What happened," Enoch said, speaking with authority and reluctance, "is, Father came home and asked Mother about a phone call he received today." Enoch turned the chair around backwards, pulled it closer to the table between Joe and Willa, and sat down. He rested his arms on the back of the chair and let his shoulders drop.

No one spoke. Even Floyd sat silent.

"Apparently Rachel's therapist called Father today at work and said the hospital would be petitioning the court for his removal as Rachel's guardian."

"Black, bigoted bitch," Floyd said.

Everyone turned shocked eyes on Floyd.

"She's insane," Floyd said, glaring at everyone. "She suggested the most evil things about me. Made them up. Pathological liar. Loony from working in a loony bin." He settled his face into a hostile stare and folded his arms across his chest. "Your mother has been telling her lies, crazy, insane lies."

"After I called you, Jessie, I put in an emergency call to Pearl Whitman. Turns out she'd been trying to call me. When I told her what had occurred at home, she sounded upset but not too surprised."

"Are you going to tell us what happened?" Jessie asked. Her voice was strained by frustration at having to wait.

"Joe," Enoch said, turning directly toward Joe. "I would appreciate your staying. I've grown to like you and trust you, but this is an ugly affair. Feel free to leave."

"You can stay," Jessie said. "I'm sure there's nothing so shocking you haven't heard it before. Besides," she paused to cast her father a sardonic look, "this is a minister's home. We don't do really bad things here."

Enoch gave Jessie an irritating look. "You may eat those words when I'm finished."

"Get on with it," Jessie said, obviously chaffed by Enoch's reprimand.

"Through discussion with Rachel, Pearl has learned she was a victim of sexual abuse."

"I knew it," Jessie interrupted. She slapped the table with an open hand. "I knew that Butch was a pervert."

Enoch shook his head no as he said, "No. Not Butch. Incest."

Hunched in her chair, traumatized by the evening's earlier events, Willa burst out crying, swaying slightly with the pulsing agony between her legs.

"Who?" Jessie screeched, jumping up from her chair and flashing accusing eyes at Enoch, her father, and then at Willa. "Tell me!"

"If you could sit down and be quiet," Enoch said, "it would be much easier for me." He reached over and patted his mother's trembling arm until she calmed a bit.

"It appears that Father treated Rachel inappropriately when she was very young, though Rachel remains somewhat cryptic about the details. However," he looked sadly at his mother, "Mother confirms it happened."

Floyd stood up, slammed his chair into the table and stormed away toward the dining room. Willa cried, "Floyd," and burst into a fresh flood of tears. He paused and turned. Folding her arms on the table, she dropped her head forward and buried her face. In a muffled voice she said, "I tried to stop him; but he hurt me." She lifted her tear-streaked face, ravaged by guilt and suffering now that truths were being revealed. She swiped at the river of tears that flowed past her trembling lips and said in a sad, pleading voice, "I loved him." She turned her long-suffering gaze on the object of her affection and saw hatred in Floyd's eyes beyond any she had seen before. She dropped her head onto her arms again and wept.

"Lying, insane bitch," Floyd said.

"Father," Enoch said as Floyd turned away. "Please come back and sit down. This isn't going to go away and we might as well finish the discussion now."

"It isn't true," Floyd said, returning to the table and dropping into his chair. "It's the fruits of Willa's wild imagination. She has a sick mind. I should have never married her. She was a nothing. I knew she would try to destroy me." He dropped his head and stared at his hands. "Perhaps she should be committed with Rachel."

The silence in the room was heavy and raw.

"The information came first from Rachel," Enoch said softly, looking at the opposite wall and speaking into the still air. "It began sometime around age three and ended when she got the thyroid disease." Enoch looked at his father with hostile and accusing eyes. "When she no longer was a beautiful child. No longer attractive to your sick, perverted mind."

Jessie and Joe exchanged embarrassed glances.

"Mother confirmed this with Pearl, causing Pearl to conclude that Father's actions are at the root of Rachel's illness. Pearl called Father today to let him know the hospital had petitioned the court for a change in guardianship."

"The whole thing's preposterous," Floyd said, looking up briefly. "I've never done anything to harm Rachel. I should be in charge of her assets. She's my daughter. I should be the one to take care of her."

Jessie and Enoch both looked at their father, wordlessly, glaring at his pompous face. Floyd glared back then returned to studying his fingernails in his lap.

"I didn't know this when I spoke with you earlier, Jessie," Enoch said. "But tonight is not the first time that father has harmed mother physically." With traces of growing awareness changing the expression in his eyes, Enoch looked at Jessie and added, "But it will be the last."

Chapter 20

The Rock of Pearl

Contrary to Enoch's expectations, Jessie didn't batter him with questions during their private talk later that evening. After helping their mother prepare for bed in the guest room, Enoch took Jessie into his father's study and offered to provide more detail. He'd assumed she would want to hear everything he knew, and he needed to share this family tragedy with another concerned family member. Also, he wanted her advice.

Enoch took a seat beside Jessie on the small leather couch and talked quietly, his face turned toward his father's empty desk as he recounted the details in a strange monotone.

As Enoch patiently explained Rachel's abuse and the brutality that had occurred in their family kitchen that night, he stole glances at Jessie. She looked depleted and unfocused, a rare circumstance for her.

"To be honest," Enoch said, turning toward Jessie and patting her hand briefly, "I feel as though my life has been turned upside-down, like I've experienced a sense of loss, much more painful than the death of someone I loved."

Jessie's quietness worried Enoch. He started to resume his discourse but Jessie stood up, cutting him short. He stared at her in surprise and confusion.

"And the point of this is…?" she asked, turning toward the door.

"I, I don't know. I thought you would want to know everything. I also wanted to ask you what you thought about my taking Mother to live with me at Rachel's house." Enoch rose to follow Jessie.

"I trust you to do the right thing," was all Jessie could say as she opened the door and headed back to the kitchen where Joe sat at the table, patiently waiting for her.

***

The ride back to Jessie's apartment in Boston that night was long. Joe played the radio softly to avoid total silence. Jessie's mind, usually calm and rational, felt like a city under attack by Godzilla. Maddening 'what ifs' flew hither and yon, tumbling over each other, crashing into buildings and scattering in a million directions.

In her search for proof that Butch had abused Rachel, she had learned of shocking events in her own family that had thrust her into emotional turmoil and enveloped her in a sense of loss for which she had no words.

Demons of doubt attacked the citadel of confidence she'd tried so hard to build since she had claimed responsibility for Butch's death. She hated uncertainty and cast about in her mind for something to restore her crumbling convictions.

Suddenly she felt consumed by a desire to be alone. She wanted to pour herself a stiff drink and fall into a deep sleep. She wanted to awake in the morning to find this had been nothing more than a bad dream and like even the most frightening monster movies, things would come out right in the end.

***

"I thought your lawyer forbade you to meet with me," were Pearl's first words as Jessie settled into the chair beside Pearl's desk the following Friday.

"He doesn't know I'm here," Jessie said.

The two women sat silently, each studying the other, neither eager to take the lead. Jessie sat with her bulging black purse clutched in her lap like a life preserver. She rhythmically tapped her fingers on the soft leather.

On the phone, Jessie had asked to see Pearl to help Rachel. In a sense, that was very true. Jessie had rationalized that by taking responsibility for Rachel's killing Butch, she was in fact doing more to help Rachel than anyone else. She owed her sister. Putting her own freedom at risk had not occurred to Jessie in the mania of the moment.

But with the passing of time and the inability of her lawyer to get the charges dropped, Jessie's brilliant plan to save her sister, conceived with impetuous and arrogant confidence, now appeared to be the worst decision in her life.

Every word out of Joe's mouth had eaten away at her smug belief in her ability to carry this scheme off successfully. Perhaps it would have been easier and less threatening if Joe were a brash, overconfident and cocky detective; but he was exactly the opposite. As her respect and affection for Joe increased, she found herself believing she was damaging their relationship irreparably by building it on the basis of a fabrication.

Maybe her affection for Joe was gnawing at her deep down. But the real cause of her eroding confidence in her ability to carry this off was—she hated to admit it even to herself—her fear of prison.

Lying awake for the past few weeks she'd suffered insecurities that had never raised their ugly heads before. She'd tried to argue that the love she felt for her sister transcended a selfish concern for herself. After all, she was strong and capable; Rachel was weak and helpless. These new revelations of abuse in Rachel's childhood, and at the hand of their own father; these were too much. Jessie would conclude she had to save Rachel from further suffering, even if it meant Jessie was convicted and sent to prison.

Then the wretched hags of her prison nightmares would reach out in the darkness and grab her with their talon-like claws. Huge wrought iron gates would slam shut behind her. Keys turned in ancient, rusty locks. Down dark and dank corridors of hell they dragged her.

As she writhed in her tangled sheets, her traumatized brain would concoct violent and twisted dreams inspired by a movie she'd seen years before about a woman who had been sentenced to prison and had been abused by guards and predatory prisoners. Scenes of bathroom attacks and fearful night tortures would wake Jessie, bathed in sweat and screaming at shadows.

This terrible beast that was closing in on her was of her own making. Now it appeared to Jessie that in order to save herself, she would have to destroy Rachel. But she couldn't. The torment to her soul was a new and strange experience. To this point in her life, Jessie's self-centered existence had caused her not one whit of concern. She had never questioned herself or her actions.

"Looks like you're having quite a contentious debate inside your head," Pearl said as she drew her eyes from the windows where she'd been gazing, patiently waiting for Jessie to speak. "Get it sorted out yet?"

"It can't be sorted out," Jessie said.

"So you have come to me with the impossible, yet your presence indicates you have maintained a ray of hope. Hope for what?"

"I'm not even sure of that," Jessie said with a hapless smile, a smile so thin it barely moved her lips. "I'm not used to not being sure."

"You said you wanted to help Rachel," Pearl reminded her. "Should we start there?"

"We can," Jessie agreed. "But the truth is, I'm the one who can destroy her. No matter what Father did, or Butch, or her pathetic little life of guilt and shame, I'm the person who can deliver the final blow, or," Jessie paused for one more short internal battle. "Or I can be her strongest protector." Jessie hesitated then finished her thought. "It's her or me, and sacrificing myself for a sister who may never come out of a mental institution seems, somehow, futile."

"Well, you have my attention. Can you paint a clearer picture for me?" Pearl leaned back in her chair to listen.

"I'll try," Jessie said. "I'll try, but I'm so confused. It all made so much more sense back on the night Rachel killed Butch."

***

When Pearl swerved to avoid being sideswiped on her drive home that evening, she gave in to her first experience of road rage, though she kept her string of curses within the confines of her car.

As she took her seat for dinner with her husband that night, she looked at the rosy rare double lamb chop on her plate and burst into tears.

"What's the matter?" her husband cried as he jumped up from his chair and ran around to hug Pearl. "Hormones? Bad day?" He took her hand and helped her up from the table. He led her into the living room where he sat her down on the couch and took her in his arms. He was tall and thin, quite the opposite from his adored wife. He held her gently and let her sobs continue until they diminished to quiet crying.

"Sometimes I wish I could bear some of the brunt of your pregnancy for you," he said into her hair. Pushing her head back so he could look into her eyes, he added with a warm smile, "Not really. I don't think men were made for this journey."

Pearl smiled in return and pulled a tissue from her skirt pocket. "I usually hand tissues to my patients," she said with a self-conscious chuckle. "You know it's not like me to cry."

"Tell me what brought this on."

"Why don't we return to eating the lovely meal you cooked and I'll explain it as best I can."

As Pearl and her husband finished the last bites of the lamb chops and oven roasted potatoes, Pearl summed up her problem, knowing that talking it out with her husband had brought relief but no solution.

"So, as a therapist, I can't reveal any of the things I was told today, even if it means the wrong person has been charged with murder and may go to prison for a crime she didn't commit. While

I thought my anger centered on the restrictions of my profession, the truth is, I am angry that this dilemma has been laid in my lap. I'm angry that I was chosen for this confidence. Yet, I know it is my job and that I had requested the sister come to me. In my efforts to help one person, I've created my own misery and must suffer accordingly."

"But she could change her mind and tell the police the truth," Pearl's husband said. "What do you think she will do?"

"I think she will ignore my advice to tell the truth and not give in to her fears. She is a stubborn and courageous young woman whose guilt for past sins, in spite of her rejection and scorn for her childhood religion, will propel her into hell, a hell of her own making."

"Perhaps she will be acquitted."

"I pray that she will."

CHAPTER 21

Diversion Into Hell

The pool of blood on Rachel's kitchen floor had dried to a hard glossy finish. Willa stared at it then at Enoch. "I've never seen this much blood before."

"Don't worry about it," Enoch said. He moved quickly from room to room, throwing windows open to let in the crisp October air while Willa donned a faded apron from the back room. In the kitchen he searched under the kitchen sink and in the utility closet for a bucket. "I'll clean it up."

"I'll help you." Willa still moved with difficulty from the pain in her pelvis.

While Willa and Enoch set the kitchen to rights and cleaned the floor, they rehashed the past week at home with Floyd and the past two days in court where Enoch had been appointed Rachel's guardian.

"Jessie surprises me," Willa said as she laid a hot detergent-soaked rag over the spidery rivulets of dried blood to soften them and scrub them away. "I never pictured her caring much about any of her family, least of all me."

"Jessie's a great girl," Enoch said. "I didn't get to know her very well while she was growing up; she was so much younger. But I've grown very fond of her lately."

"Jezebel was a handful when she was little," Willa said.

"Jezebel?" Enoch asked. "Why would you call her such an awful name?"

"I never did," Willa said. She bent forward and scrubbed vigorously at the larger pool of dried blood. "She used to write *Jezebel Keller* on all her essays in school. She said that's who she really was and that she hated the name Jessie." Willa rinsed her rag in the bucket. "Now I learn that while she was outside, and I thought she was playing with the neighbors' children, she was spying on the adults and recording every sordid incident in their lives." Willa laughed. "When she told me the other day that all the scratches she used to come home with were from sitting in bushes outside people's houses and recording what went on inside, I had to laugh. I guess she was cut out to be a reporter." Willa sat back on her heels and looked at Enoch who was refilling a bucket in the sink.

"You know, Enoch…" Tears welled up in her watery green eyes. "I have done terrible things to my children."

"You never did anything you didn't believe was right."

"Your father and I should have believed Jessie about that awful story she wrote about Rachel and that boy. But I couldn't stand up to Floyd. I knew he was doing what his parents would have done, and mine too." Willa began to cry. "Lord knows what they would have done if Floyd and I hadn't gotten married." She lifted the hem of Rachel's apron to wipe the tears away. A tiny brass key slipped out of the pocket and fell on the yellow linoleum. "What's that?" she asked in mid-sniffle.

Enoch brought the bucket of hot water over and set it down near Willa. "I'll get a scrub brush," he said.

"Enoch. Look. This fell out of Rachel's apron." She held the key up so Enoch could see it. "I wonder what it goes to."

Enoch took the tiny key and turned it in his fingers. "I bet I know," he said. He reached out his hand to help Willa stand up. She winced with pain in spite of her effort to deny it. Enoch gave her a look of understanding and said, "You're doing great, Mother. Come with me."

She followed him into the living room but remained standing while he sat down on the couch and inserted the key into the lock on Butch's family Bible.

"You mustn't open that!" Willa cried. Being calm and brave was a work in progress for Willa. The smallest thing could shatter the new persona she had resolved so courageously to develop. Apprehension shadowed her face, though her curiosity was as great as Enoch's. "Rachel said Butch never allowed her to look inside."

"Well..." Enoch looked up at his mother then back at the Bible. "Rachel is in a mental institution, and Butch is dead. And..." he lifted the heavy leather cover gently, "you and I live here now by permission of the court. So..." he spoke in broken phrases as his eyes followed his finger down the brittle page, reading out loud from the list of births, deaths and marriages. Flipping the pages back and forth in confusion, he made the same discovery that Rachel had made. No Vogels.

Unable to restrain her curiosity, Willa moved closer and sat down beside Enoch, taking a few moments to find a comfortable position. "Be careful with the pages," she warned. "They look so fragile."

"Look, Mother, no Vogels. The last date is 1910."

"There wouldn't be any Vogels," Willa explained. "If the entries stop before Butch's mother married, only her maiden name would be here."

"Move your nose back," Enoch said with a smile as he did the natural thing and began flipping through the books of the Old Testament. His bland look of curiosity was quickly banished when he came to the first picture of a little girl in a pornographic pose. He cried, "Oh, my good lord," and slammed the Bible shut, glancing in fear at his mother beside him. Composing himself he said in a more natural tone, "I hope you didn't see that picture."

Willa's eyes were wide open; her face was frozen in a mask of shock. Her hands flew up to cover her eyes. Enoch put his arm around her. "I'm sorry you saw that. I never dreamed something like that would be inside."

Willa let Enoch hold her in his arms but for once in her life, instead of crumpling into a heap of sloppy emotion, she made herself think. Sitting up straight and gently removing Enoch's arms she blinked back her tears and said, "Enoch? I think we've found something significant, significant in Rachel's life." With her pale green eyes fastened on Enoch's face she said, "We must look at this Bible more closely. Remember, the key was in Rachel's apron pocket."

"I've already put those facts together," Enoch said. "For the key to be in Rachel's pocket, it must mean she'd discovered what was in this Bible also." He looked anxiously at Willa. "Do you think you can handle this?" Willa nodded a silent yes. Enoch reopened the Bible and began flipping through the pages, looking for breaks at the splayed edges indicating the location of each photograph.

Willa sat beside Enoch unheeded tears streaming down her cheeks as she intently followed Enoch's motions. Each picture that Enoch found intensified the pain gripping Willa's heart.

"Oh, Enoch," Willa cried out clamping her hands on his arm like the claws of an eagle. "Oh, Enoch." Enoch turned and looked into his mother's face, noting the wrinkles that were becoming more deeply etched over the past few months.

"What?"

"That's little Charlotte!" Willa's voice had risen to a skinny shriek as she tried to stifle verbalizing the shocking revelation.

"Charlotte who?"

"The little girl who lives upstairs."

The silence that fell between them served better than words allowing them each to process their thoughts privately.

At last Willa spoke. "Rachel must have found these pictures. Poor Rachel." Willa rose painfully and looked hauntingly around the room. She walked over and touched a dusty ceramic bird with her finger. She repositioned all three figurines so the birds faced the window. She returned to her place on the couch. She was shaking. "I wonder what went on here the day Butch died."

Enoch rose from the couch and walked around the living room for a few minutes. His glances toward Willa were puzzled, as though he didn't readily recognize the person sitting on the couch.

"What is it you want?" Willa asked.

"I want to tell you something, but I don't want to hurt you further." He dropped into the chair across from Willa. "I wish I knew how strong you are because I'm beginning to see reserves in you I didn't know you had." He shook his head with the weight of all that had happened since July. "I wish I knew how much I should tell you and where I should stop."

"Enoch?" Willa said, gingerly pushing her plump body farther back on the couch and looking him straight in the eye. "I will tell you the answer to that." She took a deep breath and again, wiped the remaining tears on the hem of Rachel's apron. "There is much I need to learn, about myself and about my children. There is much that I have done wrong, ways in which I've let myself down and let my family down, too many ways to count. But, I promise you this: I will learn. I will come to understand. I will not go back to the life I lived." She paused to gain better control over her voice. "I've left your father and I shall not return." Still looking straight into Enoch's eyes she said, "So what is it you want to tell me? I can handle it."

Enoch rose again and paced the carpet, jabbing his toe at a crinkled fern in the pattern. Finally he looked at his mother and said, "Joe is convinced that Jessie did not kill Butch."

"She says she did, accidentally, I mean." Surprise tinged with hope filled Willa's eyes. "If she didn't kill him, who else could have?"

"Joe believes that Rachel killed Butch, not Jessie."

"Oh!" Willa exclaimed, her eyes falling on the tooled leather Bible with its wide strap lying open on the coffee table. "Oh."

Willa's expression changed to one of confusion. She looked up at Enoch. "Why would Jessie lie about killing Butch? Why would she say she did it if she didn't?"

"I don't know," Enoch said, dropping into the chair again. "I don't know. Joe is adamant about it."

"The papers all said Jessie's fingerprints were found on the murder weapon, not Rachel's. Doesn't that prove who did it?"

"The DA and everyone else believe it does. Joe doesn't."

"What does Joe think?"

"Joe doesn't share all of his thoughts with me, but he never stops questioning the evidence until all his questions are answered. He's seen cases where evidence pointed in the wrong direction."

"Well…I…don't know what to think." Wonder and confusion shaded Willa's subdued voice. "I don't know what to believe." She smoothed the wrinkles in Rachel's apron and resumed speaking, her voice filled with trepidation.

"Enoch. I know this may sound odd coming from me. You know I kept Floyd's cruelty a secret all these years." Shame washed over Willa's face but she plowed on with her question. "I was wondering, do you know anything bad about Rachel's marriage, you know, anything personal about it? Like how he treated her, how she really felt toward him, whether they fought or not?" Enoch looked at Willa but didn't respond. "Jessie says Butch physically abused Rachel. But everyone in church appeared to like Butch. He was always friendly, helped out with projects, like painting and repairs, even came over and helped Floyd with things at our house when Floyd asked. I know Floyd liked him. And he was always polite and considerate to me. Thanked me for meals and offered to help wash the dishes, things like that. He seemed nice enough."

"What do we ever know about people, really know about them?" Pain crept into Enoch's dark green eyes as he framed the question.

"I know," Willa said, intuiting Enoch's thoughts about his own experience and understanding her own more clearly. "For so many years I was the only person who knew about Floyd's dark side. I refused to see the truth. I wanted things to be the way I wanted them to be." She shifted her position and looked at Enoch. "Do you ever think about Leah?"

"Sometimes." Enoch released a soft sigh. "Maybe Butch was as much a fraud as Leah and Father. Look at those pictures." Enoch indicated Butch's Bible. "Decent men don't collect pictures like that."

Enoch leaned forward and rested his elbows on his knees. "I need to think this through. Butch never held a job for any length of time. I know he gambled because they busted up a group of guys at a local beer hall and Butch was involved."

"Was Butch arrested for gambling?" Willa asked.

"It never came to that. Two of the guys involved were cops."

"I know Butch pressured Rachel to ask for a raise," Willa said. "She mentioned it last winter, just before Christmas, while she was helping me with dinner. Said she was uncomfortable asking for another raise, now that she was promoted to office manager. Said they'd already given her a raise with the increased responsibility and was sure there was no chance of more."

"What else did she say?"

"Said Butch blamed her for his failure to build that supplemental food business. He told her that if she'd had more money for him to put into the deal, he'd have been successful." Willa shook her head as she contested her daughter's belief. "I didn't agree with her, but Rachel was concerned that her inability to earn more was harming Butch's chances at success. That's what she was worried about."

Willa rose from the couch, fixing her eyes on the Bible as though it were a cobra poised to strike. "I must call Pearl and tell her about these pictures." She looked at Enoch as she headed for the kitchen. "She'll know what to do."

***

"You found these where?" Joe asked Enoch as he dumped the large envelope of pornographic pictures out on his desk and flipped through them. "That Bible on the coffee table?" Joe slipped some smaller Polaroids from a white envelope.

"Those are of the little girl who lives upstairs," Enoch said. "Mother recognized her."

Joe pushed the photographs away in disgust. "The world will suffer no loss with Butch's death," he said. He leaned back in his chair and studied Enoch, sitting across his desk. "You are right; they aren't evidence for the case. They have nothing to do with Jessie. But…and here's where I believe the big but is…I think these are evidence pointing toward Rachel's killing Butch." Joe got up and closed the door to his small office. Returning to his seat he grabbed the pictures into a heap and stuffed them back into the envelope. "Let me get this straight. Your mother found the key in an apron Rachel had probably worn the day Butch died. Right?"

"I would assume that."

"From what I learned at your parents' house last week," Joe dropped his voice even lower, "this could have been a deadly trigger for Rachel's emotions based on her childhood experience. To find that her husband harbored the same evil in his mind that her own father had perpetrated on her."

"I see where you're going," Enoch said, ill at ease and shifting in his chair. "Could it have been the last straw for Rachel?"

"I don't know," Joe said, pressing his fingers together to form a ball. "I don't know. But I bet I know who does." He looked at Enoch earnestly and asked, "Am I making this unbearable for you? Both of these women are your sisters."

"Joe?" Enoch said, dropping his foot to the floor and leaning forward. "At this point, all I care about is that no one gets hurt any more, ever." He leaned back in the chair and let his head tilt backwards until it touched the Venetian blinds inside the windows of Joe's office. "I grew up thinking that my family was a good family, that I was lucky to be raised by parents who were devoted to God and who took care of us, sending us to school and college, and making sure we were prepared for lives of our own. But from A to Z, reality proves that our family is a disaster, a pool of tragedy, all of us living and suffering alone, no one being able to help the other. Now, all I want, if I want anything, is for Rachel to get well, for Mother to continue to grow stronger and become a real person, and for Jessie to be found not guilty."

Enoch stood to leave Joe's office. "Do we have to report the little girl upstairs?"

Joe looked at Enoch knowing he was not trying to skirt the law, only save a child and her parents from extreme pain. "I don't know. I'll check with Tinker. I'll let you know." Enoch reached for the doorknob. "Enoch?" Enoch turned. "I'm more convinced than ever that Jessie didn't do it. Frankly, I believe that Rachel was driven to it. I feel it in my gut; I just need proof."

CHAPTER 22

Drawing Water from the Earth

Therapists who work with victims of incest know and understand the anxiety that plagued Pearl each time she sat down with Rachel. So many evils were enacted on innocent children by those they trusted, it fatigued Pearl to think about it. Of all the things she'd studied and observed through her professional experience, incest was truly the most damaging.

However, she told herself in her private moments, there were hundreds, thousands of people, victims of incest, who were able to lead reasonably ordinary lives, though we never know the truth behind most. Rachel appeared to be resilient.

Pearl sipped a lukewarm cup of coffee, let her eyes rest on the view beyond the wrought iron fence and switched her mental meanderings to Willa. Now there is an amazing woman, she told herself. Willa was much like the tree, the willow tree, weeping and bending in the storm, but resilient and providing great comfort with its serene beauty. Someday, Pearl fully believed, Willa would be that serene and beautiful person.

But today, it's Rachel I must help, Pearl told herself. She carefully read the ward supervisor's report. As she restored the file to order, the orderly arrived with Rachel.

"You look rested," Pearl said to Rachel. "Please sit down."

"I feel rested," Rachel said, taking her seat and relaxing her hands in her lap. "I slept through most of the night, except when Ellen or Betsy were snoring too loudly." She smiled.

"Well, Rachel?" Pearl began. "What shall we sing today?"

"I love that hymn about the old rugged cross."

As they had been doing three times a week since mid-September, Pearl and Rachel sang together. Rachel's voice had lost its childish and cracked quality, smoothing into the soft but lovely voice of a woman, too fragile to enhance a choir, but pleasant to hear. With the singing had come a slow but steady return to reality, now very near to the present, or at least the current year when Rachel had begun to slide into exhaustion from lack of sleep.

Expertly leading Rachel back into the final thoughts of their last session, Pearl said, "So it was February that you began to feel tired and depressed?"

"Yes," Rachel answered. Her voice was soft but firm. As was her habit, she steadied her gaze on Pearl's face from which she drew inner strength like the skies drawing water up from the earth. "I couldn't sleep at night, but I always went to work and maintained all my responsibilities. It was just harder because I was so tired."

"Why couldn't you sleep?" Pearl asked.

"Because of my guilty conscience."

"You mentioned you felt guilty last week. Are you ready to tell me why you felt so guilty you couldn't sleep?"

"I was stealing." Rachel dropped her eyes to her lap, cutting off her source of strength from Pearl. "I was embezzling."

"Can you tell me why such an honest and dedicated employee like you would embezzle from your employer?"

Rachel looked up at Pearl, locked her eyes on Pearl's face and began her story.

"For years my husband had demanded that I earn more money even if that meant changing jobs or changing my type of work. He told me there was no point in staying at a dead-end job where I wasn't appreciated and was underpaid. That was slavery.

"I tried to tell him that I loved my job, my employer was very nice to me and that I felt appreciated. Lawyers are an interesting bunch of people, but I rarely interacted with most of them. In the office, we did all the bookkeeping, time tracking, billing, payroll, and managed the trust accounts, you know, the business stuff.

"When they offered me the office manager's position," Rachel paused to count on her fingers. "I'm sorry, I've lost track of time. It must have been around August of last year. They gave me a considerable raise commensurate with my increased responsibilities and level of trust. I was thrilled. I couldn't get home fast enough to tell Butch."

"What did Butch say?"

"He seemed very pleased. Then he made me list all of my responsibilities, in detail, three times." Rachel smiled at Pearl. "I thought he was so proud of me he couldn't hear enough."

"Was that the case?"

"Now I believe it was not," Rachel said. "After Thanksgiving last year, Butch told me to ask for a raise. He told me every day. Every day when I'd come home from work, he'd ask me if I'd received a raise."

"What was Butch doing at that time?"

"Butch was discouraged because he'd lost out on a great business opportunity with a friend."

"Tell me about it."

"He'd met a guy who sold nutritional food supplements. His name was Rich. He joked about his name because he said anyone who joined the program would be rich, just like him."

"Was he rich?"

"I don't know. I only met him once." Rachel looked out the window and back at Pearl. "I never wanted to be rich, just comfortable. Anyway, Butch invested in a huge supply of the food supplements and told me we'd be rich as soon as he'd signed up other sales representatives to work for him."

"And?" Pearl was getting itchy, sitting there with her mouth shut. She hated pyramid schemes with a passion and here she had to sit and listen to one more victim relate their story. Instead of blurting out her feelings, Pearl asked, "What happened?"

"At first Butch tried to find other people to sell the products. Nobody was very interested. He even set up some sales people with free inventories, from his own supply. Nothing worked. Pretty soon he gave up and sat around at home. He'd be eating breakfast when I left for work and he'd be watching television when I got home from work, feeling bored and angry with me for not earning enough money." With a pained expression Rachel admitted what sounded like a breach of marital confidence. "I was supporting us both."

"Where did Butch get the money to make his initial investment?"

"He emptied our savings account, plus he took that year's Christmas club money."

"So it's nearing Christmas; you haven't received a raise; and Butch is pressuring you every day?" Pearl asked. "How did he pressure you?"

A slight but perceptible shiver passed through Rachel's shoulders. She looked away.

"Butch was verbal. But he never stopped with just words. I would listen patiently. I had promised to love and obey him and I tried my very best. But, it was never enough. He would become agitated and upset with my faults. He would remind me how I'd let him down in every way a woman could let a man down." She returned her eyes to Pearl's face. "I'd sit quietly while he lectured me. Even when he'd yell at me, I wouldn't argue back. Then, unsatisfied with words, he would pop me on the side of the head with his open hand until my ears rang and waves of pain ricocheted through my head."

"In what other ways did Butch convey his anger?"

"Sometimes I'd wake up at night with a pillow over my face, fighting for air. He'd pull the pillow away and laugh at me saying,

'Now you know what life was like in 'Nam. Better sleep with one eye open.'"

Pearl shifted her position, attempting to cross one fat leg over the other then giving up because the leg wouldn't stay in place. "Anything else?"

"He wasn't always mean to me; he was nice sometimes." Rachel looked down at her hands, an obvious wave of guilt washing over her sad face. "It's not Christian to say bad things about people." She smoothed the skirt of her dress and continued. "Usually if he was angry at me and yelling at me, he'd shove me around, you know, knocking me into things, tables, walls, chairs. When I'd try to run out of his reach, he'd grab my arm and twist it behind my back."

"Did he do that often?"

Rachel looked up. "Yes. He would hold my arm, pushing my hand upward toward my shoulder blade so it hurt, not much, just enough to make me cry. Then while he yelled at me behind my head, he'd slowly press upward on my arm until I screamed. Until I buckled and fell down, he'd keep pressing." She paused and thought a moment.

"One time I started screaming before he'd really hurt me but he knew I was faking it. He laughed at me and wrenched my arm upwards until it touched the back of my neck. I thought he'd ripped it out of its socket. I screamed and passed out."

"So you learned to never scream more than the pain demanded."

"Yes. I learned to react strictly in line with the degree of pain he caused. He taught me that. It was like a test in honesty, even when he was hurting me."

Pearl turned her head away and dabbed at her eyes with a tissue. She could never predict what could tear at her heartstrings; this lesson in honesty had been a new twist.

She turned back to Rachel. "Tell me what happened when you didn't get the raise."

"As I told you, Butch was pressuring me every day to ask. So I told him I'd asked and been refused. He hit me saying that I'd lied, that I'd never asked for the raise because I was a chicken shit little wimp who didn't think I deserved the air I breathed." Rachel grabbed her own tissue and blew her nose.

"The week before Christmas, I came home and told Butch I'd received a raise, a special Christmas surprise, and that after January, I'd begin earning another hundred dollars per week."

"What really happened?"

"I knew the annual audit would cover transactions for the current year of 1975. So after 1976 began, I started writing myself checks for one hundred dollars from the trust funds. The firm has about two hundred trust funds they manage. Many of them are inactive, meaning the people who own the money don't need it so nothing much happens during the year. I would replace the money I took from one account with money from another account. I continued on that plan until I couldn't sleep and I wanted my life to end." Rachel's eyes popped open wide and she exclaimed, "Not really." Facing Pearl in fear she added quickly, "I didn't really want to kill myself. I'm not crazy you know. I just wanted to go back and undo what I'd done, but I couldn't."

"I know you're not crazy," Pearl said, reaching over and patting Rachel's hand. "I'm sure of that. I'm also sure you must have been suffering more than you could handle. I'm sure that stealing is the last thing you wanted to do."

"But I did it," Rachel said. "I stole one hundred dollars every week and put it into our checking account. When I wrote out our check for tithe to the church every month, I always included that money when I calculated our tithe. You know, you owe ten percent of your gross income to the church. No matter how you earn it, ten percent is the Lord's money."

Pearl smiled but made no comment.

CHAPTER 23

Like Son, Like Father

"Sorry the gravy's so thick," Willa said, as she passed the gravy boat around the dining room table. "I'm still not used to cooking in Rachel's kitchen." She looked around the table at Enoch, Jessie and Joe. "I'm just making excuses."

"None of us is used to his life these last few months," Enoch said. "I still can't imagine Thanksgiving dinner without Father and Rachel."

"How is Father doing?" Jessie asked as she passed the bowl of mashed potatoes. "Not that I care all that much."

"He's silent and angry," Enoch said. "When I went over last week with the movers to get Mother's organ, he barred our entry. I should say he made a feeble attempt. He's very angry."

"Because his punching bag has escaped?" Jessie took some stuffing and passed the bowl to Joe. "There is something terribly sick about people who perpetrate evil under the cloak of righteousness. Frankly, myself, I prefer an out-and-out criminal, a person who lets you know danger is near, a man wielding a knife with sunshine glinting off the blade. At least in that instance, you know you're in trouble."

"You always had a preference for the dramatic," Willa said, giving Jessie a smile. "I knew I was in danger, down deep where I stuffed the information. But I couldn't let myself admit that I'd married a cruel and hateful man. I wanted to believe that our unfortunate car accident had created an opening to a wonderful

188

and loving life for me. All my young life I'd dreamed of marrying a handsome man, devoted to God, a man who would raise a family with me and be my soul mate, my shield, my love. I honestly thought God had dumped him right into my lap." Willa smiled again faintly. "Sometimes our childish dreams take us down perilous paths, blindfolded and naive. Perhaps only terrible events can remove our blinders and allow us to see clearly." She looked with sadness and longing at the people around her. "I wish Rachel could be here."

"I talked to Pearl today," Enoch said. "Rachel is making progress."

"Will she be able to testify?" Joe asked. So far he'd eaten in silence. "Did you ask her that?"

"This is in complete confidence," Enoch said. "She is showing increased normalcy. They don't have to sing their way through the whole session any more."

"What's confidential about that?" Jessie asked.

"There's more. Rachel has told Pearl some things about Butch, speaking of him as though he is alive, but Rachel has never asked about Butch, never questioned why he hasn't visited, or called her. Pearl doesn't think that Rachel knows Butch is dead. Rachel expresses no curiosity about him at all."

"Probably because she saw me kill him," Jessie murmured.

"She's going to broach the subject soon."

Silence reigned for a few minutes while each person ate and mulled their private thoughts.

Enoch looked at Jessie. "Pearl's pretty confident that Rachel will never be able to recall what happened in the kitchen that night. She thinks Rachel may have lost those memories in the onset of shock," Enoch said. "Like an electric outlet that shorts out and burns up the wires."

"Or she's trying to protect me," Jessie said. "Maybe she doesn't want to have to testify against her own sister."

Joe chewed on his dark turkey meat and studied Jessie's face.

Jessie kept her eyes on her plate while she chased a few green peas among the piles of squash and stuffing. Finally she stabbed the peas with her fork. "Gotcha," she said to the peas and popped them into her mouth. She brushed her large hoop earrings free of her hair as she looked up triumphantly at Joe's intent face and grinned.

Willa took another warm roll from the basket and split it open to butter it. "I've been praying that Rachel will be home for Christmas. Enoch and I can make her home so inviting for her and I think it would do her a world of good." Willa looked over at Enoch with love in her eyes. "Living here with Enoch, just the peace and comfort, has been healing for me. Until you leave hell, you don't know how awful it is."

"I admire your strength, Mother," Jessie said. "I didn't think you had that kind of courage."

"I know you didn't; I didn't either."

Joe's pager disrupted the tranquil domestic scene. He excused himself from the table and went to the kitchen to call the station.

"I have to report immediately," Joe said when he returned to the dining room. "I'm sorry I can't help clean up. There's been a fire; two people dead; they think it was set."

Out of habit Jessie jumped up. She looked at Joe and sat down again.

"Thought you were going to follow me?" Joe asked with a laugh. "Walk me to the door. I'll check in with you later tonight and give you all the details though I don't know what use they'll be to you."

Jessie had that just-been-kissed look when she returned to her chair but was obviously a little put out. "It's one thing to have crime interrupt my Thanksgiving dinner," she groused. "It's another thing to not be able to go out and get the story."

"Still have to sit in the corner everyday?" Enoch asked. They'd grown closer over the past few months and Enoch, a little belatedly, had taken on the role of a teasing older brother. Jessie shot back a few caustic remarks but it was obvious to Willa that these two siblings had grown fond of each other. That thought added to Willa's nascent contentment.

***

When Jessie returned to her apartment after helping her mother wash up the dishes, she felt happy and empty at the same time. Her thoughts were focused on the idea that she might have found her life's love in Joe. Though she faced trial for murder, she tried to force herself to believe things would turn out okay. But her darker moments still found her terrified and writhing in the emotional pits of hell.

Irrational fears plagued her night and day; the trial was only a week away. Wrapped in a fog of vacillation between hope and despair Jessie fumbled her keys and dropped them on the granite steps outside the door to her apartment building. She didn't see the man hiding in the shadows on the other side of the two pillars that framed the entrance. Nor did she take note of his following her into the building and secreting himself behind a wooden screen that gave privacy to the public phone on the wall.

Still distracted, she entered the elevator, punched the button for the fifth floor, and leaned back against the old mahogany panels as the ancient elevator inched upwards. Inside the left elevator, she couldn't see the progress of the right elevator. One or the other was usually out of order. It wasn't something a tenant thought about.

The first moment that Jessie noticed the man was when she felt a brutal push in the small of her back as she unlocked her apartment door and was shoved inside, shoved so hard she fell flat on her face. She heard her door slam behind her and heard the deadbolt click as she jumped to her feet and twisted around.

At the sight of the disheveled man standing in her apartment, she let out a shriek and ran for the phone in her kitchen.

"Not so fast, missy," the man snarled, sprinting behind her and grabbing her coat. She tried to wiggle out of her coat, but he threw his right arm around her neck and began to choke her, not enough to kill her, just enough to subdue her.

"Who are you?" Jessie screamed. "What do you want?"

His breath, smelling of alcohol and old vomit, pushed past her face like a fetid sewer. A wave of nausea brought weakness to her knees as she flailed outwards with her arms, succeeding only in beating the air. She tried kicking backwards but lost her balance. He dragged her to her feet by the neck.

"Quite the little tiger, aren't you?" the stinking man said.

Jessie clawed at the arm that encircled her throat but he pulled it tighter. "If you calm down I'll tell you why I'm here."

"Get out!" Jessie screamed, still fighting and flailing. She tried jabbing backwards with her elbows but the ragged coat and loose clothes on the man holding her acted as a buffer.

He tightened his grip on her throat and with his free hand, wrenched her head sideways, nearly twisting it off her neck. "Settle down, missy, if you want to live."

He held her firmly in that position, tightening his grip when she struggled and relaxing it a fraction when she stopped. Every time she resumed fighting, he wrenched her head tighter. Finally she stopped fighting and he said, "I have an offer you can't refuse. If you stop fighting me, I'll let you sit down so we can negotiate like gentlemen." He snickered at the misnomer and relaxed his hold, slightly.

It was obvious to Jessie she was totally ineffective in her current position. No matter what method she would use to save herself, it wasn't going to happen in this death lock.

"All right," Jessie said through a now parched and traumatized throat. Her voice sounded alien to her. "I'll sit down."

Slowly the man released his grip, stepping back from Jessie as he removed the arm around her throat. "I'll kill you if you try anything," he said calmly. "It wouldn't spoil my day."

With every bone in Jessie's body, she longed to run for the kitchen but she decided to use her wits; obviously her brawn was inferior to this animal's.

"Who are you?" she demanded as she dropped stiffly into the nearest chair in her small living room. The man remained standing, not three feet from her.

"I thought I'd let you guess," he said through broken teeth. Now that she could see his face clearly, he looked like all the bums she'd seen in the park or cowering in doorways, lying in their vomit, cheap whiskey bottles tucked in their arms. It was hard to distinguish his skin color through the crusty beard and layers of filth on his face. His eyes were rheumy and red-veined. His hair stood up in matted, gray tufts.

She glanced over his thin body draped in loose-fitting rags under a stained and buttonless overcoat. Something about his face bore a familiar aspect, but she could not place it.

"Do I know you?" she asked. She was devoting her thoughts to escape but needed to pretend she was giving him full consideration.

"Not exactly."

"Do you intend to tell me who you are and why you are here?" Jessie asked.

The man blew his nose into one of his filthy hands and wiped the mucus down the front of his coat.

Jessie almost heaved her Thanksgiving dinner.

"I'm Lester Vogel. Name mean anything to you?"

Jessie started in her chair but she calmed herself and sorted through the few details she knew about Rachel's husband's family.

"Are you Butch's father?" she asked. "Your name might have been listed in the obituary for Butch, but I can't recall it."

"Can you recall killing my son?" Lester Vogel took a step closer and leaned down nearer to Jessie's face. His stench took her breath away.

"How come you waited this long to find me?" Jessie asked. Rather a stupid question she thought but she needed time to think.

"I didn't know Butch was dead until one of my friends read an article from a newspaper that I was arranging in an alley to take a nap."

"How long have you known?" Jessie asked.

"Found out yesterday. It's taken me a day to get sober enough to find your address. I'm doing fine now, aren't I?" He took a few steps backward and sat down on the edge of a plaid hassock.

I'll have to give that to Goodwill, Jessie mused. Probably be infested with lice and fleas.

"What do you want?" Jessie wanted to jump up and run. She considered diving out the elegant windows of her old-fashioned living room. Probably kill myself. She pictured the wrought iron railing that ran around the entry to the sublevel apartments of the building. Probably land on Old Mrs. Tuesday letting in her cat.

The filthy man facing her appeared harmless at first glance, which tortured her with her weakness until she tried to clear her throat and the pain nearly choked her. I should be handling this much better she told herself. Where is my ingenuity? Where are my Nancy Drew instincts?

Leering at her with his slack-lipped mouth where spittle hovered in sticky globs at the corners, Lester Vogel said, "I want money."

"For what?" Jessie reacted with surprise and sarcasm. "What makes you think I'm going to give you money?"

"You killed my son. The paper said you're standing trial for his murder. I know you're going to be convicted. You've admitted to killing Butch." Lester paused to reorder his thoughts. The struggle to think clearly was evident in his eyes. You could almost see his thoughts fading into darkness then returning to the light as he arranged his words with slow deliberation.

"Before they send you to jail, I want the money I would win in an unlawful death suit."

"What do you know about unlawful death suits?" Jessie asked. "I'd assume you're more an expert on bar stools or park benches."

"I was a lawyer once," Lester said, dropping his head slightly. Jessie thought that through the filth and stubble she could detect a slight expression of shame.

"Then you know that you have to process a suit before you get any money. If you were a lawyer, and if you knew the facts of your son's death, you would know that I will be acquitted." She pushed the last words out as though she could push him out of the room.

Then it struck her: words weren't the answer; she needed to take action. There was a way out. All she had to do was be very, very clever and very, very careful.

Jessie rose from her chair to reach for her purse. Lester lunged at her and attacked her, knocking her to the floor, his infested body landing on top of her. She screamed. He clamped his putrid hand over her mouth and with the other hand, wrenched her left arm around behind her back, pressing upwards rapidly and with great strength.

Jessie screamed with pain and blacked out for a few moments. When she came to, she was still on the floor and Lester was crouched beside her, still pinning her to the floor by the arm twisted behind her back.

"Thought you were going somewhere, missy?" Lester asked.

With her face pressed against the polished hardwood floor, Jessie gulped for breath and tried to speak, though terror now hovered at the edges of her mind. "I was just going to get my purse."

"You need to ask permission, missy," Lester said. "You mustn't surprise Old Lester. It makes him nervous."

"I was going to see how much cash I had in my purse."

Lester laughed, a ghoulish, mucus laden, guttural sound of humorless mirth. "Cash, missy? You think I'm going to settle for the cash in your purse?" Lester released her arm and stood up. "Get your purse and get back in your chair," he commanded. "Let's talk."

Jessie pulled her purse into her lap and sat down again. She

195

had lost her sense of composure and had begun to tremble, starting with the arm that was lacerated with pain, then her legs. Even her teeth were chattering.

"What I want is every penny you have, missy." Lester took a seat facing her and dropped his hands on his knees. "It's easy. Just open your purse and hand me your savings passbook and a signed blank check on your checking account."

"You can't get away with this," Jessie said. "You'll need identification. You can't withdraw money that easily." Jessie's legs were vibrating with fear.

"You'd be surprised the miracles that some of my friends can work," Lester said. The sneering voice raised the hairs on the back of Jessie's neck.

"Okay," Jessie said, appearing to give in to his demands. "Okay, I'll give you the money. If I do, will you leave me alone?"

"After I tie you up so you can't muck up my plans." His grin was soulless. "Someone will find you in a few days, maybe." He wiped his filthy mouth with the back of his hand.

The small Derringer that lay in the bottom of Jessie's purse had always struck her as slightly foolish, more danger to herself than any attacker. She knew the scorn most cops felt for people who carried guns but didn't have the skill to use them. Suddenly its minute size and proven talent for slowing down a dangerous person made perfect sense. Positive when she'd applied for her gun license that she'd never need it, Jessie now felt a cool stream of resolve pass through her gut, up to her shoulders and down her trembling arms. As she slowly placed her hand into her purse, Lester's eyes followed every muscle twitch.

"Make sure you don't surprise Old Lester," he said. "You know how that upsets me."

Slick as a professional gunslinger in an old black-and-white western, Jessie retrieved the pistol and pulled the trigger as the muzzle cleared the lip of her purse. The sound of the gunshot ricocheted around the walls of her living room as the wasted piece of human excrement toppled face down on the floor.

Jessie didn't wait to see if he was alive or dead. She ran. She burst out of her apartment screaming and ran to the stairs, bypassing the antediluvian elevators. She ran howling down one flight after the other.

She had lost track of time since she had unlocked her apartment door and now was shocked back into reality when she fell into Joe's arms as she slammed out of the apartment building door.

On the verge of hysteria, Jessie crumpled into Joe's arms and cried, "I killed him! I killed him!"

"I've heard that before," Joe said as he gently backed her into the lobby and held her away from him enough to see her face. "I don't know what's happened to you, but your dramatic skills have definitely improved." Joe smiled affectionately and took her in his arms. "What the heck is going on?"

To Joe's surprise, Jessie was really trembling and couldn't stop crying.

"Come over here and sit down," Joe said, leading Jessie to a small cluster of chairs in front of a cold fireplace.

"He could still be alive!" Jessie cried in breathless gasps. "He might be coming down the stairs right now!"

"Who?" Joe began to take Jessie seriously.

"Butch's father! I shot him!"

CHAPTER 24

Bits and Pieces

Jessie walked into her editor's glass-paneled office, closed the door and sat down.

"I take it you have a death wish," her boss said, carelessly dropping the ash from his cigar beside the ashtray. "First the son and then the father. Anything special about that family we should know?" Jessie stared at the cigar ash and did not respond. She hated the stink of cigars but today she hardly noticed the foul smell.

"I think you need to take some time off. Your trial starts on Wednesday, your first trial, that is. I'm putting you on leave of absence until all these murders get squared away."

Jessie rose and turned toward the door.

In an entirely different tone the editor said, "I'm sorry we couldn't keep it off the front page, too many unique twists at this point." He paused and threw the morning's paper on a heap of older issues on the floor beside his chair. "I'm sorry for what's happening in your life right now, Jessie. I'd rather have you as my star reporter than as the star suspect in every murder in the Greater Boston area." Jessie grabbed the brushed nickel door handle. "I'll have Cathleen cover the trial. She's our best on the court beat. I want you to call me every day. If there's any way I can help you, let me know."

***

Jessie had barely taken a seat in her lawyer's office when Ben began. "Do you confess to every murder that happens this side of the Mississippi?" Ben Levine's shoulders drooped and he let his head sag with the weight of his bewilderment at Jessie.

Jessie squirmed in her chair and tried to buy a few moments while she studied the diplomas on Ben's wall. Tears formed in the corners of her eyes, uncharacteristic for her, and distressing to her self-confidence. "I shot him. He was going to kill me." Her voice trembled as she looked Ben in the eye.

"This time I believe you," Ben said. "I notice you don't have your notes at the ready; memory serving you better?"

The sarcasm in Ben's voice triggered the old Jessie. "My memory's fine, thank you."

"Well, your sister's isn't," Ben said. He let out a breath of exasperation with the young woman sitting in front of his desk. "Your appointment with me today was to finalize the details of your trial and go over our strategy."

"What about what happened last Thursday?" Jessie asked. "Will you defend me or not?"

"I was glad to help you at the arraignment on Friday, but at this point, I'd like to stay focused on one dead body at a time. I'll have one of my partners take the case under advisement and work through the initial investigative processes. I'd like to make my final decision when we finish this trial. Is that acceptable to you?"

"Yes," Jessie said, breathing a sigh of relief.

"For one thing," Ben said, "I'm glad the second incident didn't happen in that Detective D'nardo's jurisdiction."

"Why?" Jessie asked, looking up at Ben in surprise. "What's wrong with him?"

"I think he's playing a dangerous game. I only hope he doesn't fuck up the trial."

"What do you mean? What has he done?"

"He's pressuring Rachel's therapist to permit Rachel to testify in court. He's called here twice to talk to me. He knows damned well he can't do that." As an aside, Ben added, "He's not prosecuting this case."

Jessie let the discussion of Joe drop. Though he appeared to love her and believe she was incapable of killing anyone, last Thursday night had been a shock to their relationship.

Once Joe had understood what had happened, he'd taken over and acted as her protector, doing his best to handle the police while keeping the appropriate distance required. He'd gone with her to the police station and arranged for bail so she could stay with Willa and Enoch at Rachel's house, thus avoiding another night in a jail cell. In language that cut to the chase, Joe had provided the essential facts surrounding Butch's death and assured the arresting officer that this man, Butch's father, was a valueless human being and certainly had no good intentions.

For the first time since Jessie had met Joe, she felt he believed her, every single word. When she and Joe had hashed over the two murders during the past weekend, she also felt that Joe was interrogating her, with far more hostility than a lawyer trying to impeach an unreliable witness. Something was bugging Joe and try as he might to dismiss it, it hung in the air between them like the smell of skunk at a picnic.

Jessie smirked at her odiferous simile and turned her attention back to Ben who had finished writing some notes on a yellow pad. He was staring at her expectantly.

"Ready to get to work? We've got only two days until trial."

***

Pearl sang softly with Rachel, longing for the light to come back into Rachel's eyes, like the week before. They sang "This Little Light of Mine." It was like a touchstone to the good things in Rachel's childhood. Then they sang "The Old Rugged Cross," a song that reached deep into Rachel's more mature psyche, lending pensiveness to her face that changed to faint flickers of courage.

During their first session of the prior week Pearl had told Rachel that Butch was dead. She had startled Rachel and was not surprised that Rachel had immediately regressed in memory and speech. Though Pearl had avoided the details, including the manner of his death, it appeared that Rachel was running away from that night, away from people and events that were too terrifying to recall.

The following two sessions had been spent in helping Rachel restore her confidence in speaking with Pearl. They'd talked about Rachel's college years and worked their way up to the Christmas she'd met Butch.

Today, Pearl needed to continue chipping away at that carapace of fear and see if she could peek beneath it. She wasn't even sure if Rachel had accepted that Butch was dead.

"Your voice sounds lovely today," Pearl said by way of opening their conversation. Pearl looked at the snowy scene beyond her windows. "Did you see that it snowed last night? It was beautiful driving to work this morning."

Rachel looked out the window and smiled.

"Yes. It is beautiful." She looked back at Pearl and said, "Perhaps I can walk outside this afternoon."

"Rachel," Pearl began. "Last week you were telling me that you and Butch met in December 1966, and that he joined you and your family for Christmas." Rachel nodded agreement. "Christmas isn't far away. Have you given thought to spending Christmas with your family?"

"Not Butch."

"Why not Butch?"

"Because Butch is gone."

"Where do you think Butch is right now?"

"In hell." Rachel's response surprised Pearl.

"Why do you think he's in hell?"

Rachel looked down at her hands and twisted her fingers into a fleshy knot. "Because of his mother's Bible."

"Could you tell me why his mother's Bible would place him in hell?"

"Because of the pictures."

"What kind of pictures?"

"Bad pictures. Very bad pictures." Rachel raised her eyes revealing an intense feeling of guilt. "I looked in the Bible. I found Butch's key and I looked inside." Her expression changed to anger and she spoke softly. "Butch is dead." With vehemence she added, "He is in hell."

Putting a patient's story fragments into order and gleaning the truth was something Pearl did extremely well. She had filled in the gaps many times and had been correct. Sometimes the vagaries of the mind, when confused with religious teachings or fantasies, were more puzzling.

"Tell me about Butch's Bible. Did you and Butch read the Bible together?"

"No." Rachel spoke with slow deliberation. Her fingers were knotted more tightly, cutting off the blood at the joints and turning the skin ghastly white as she starved the fingertips for blood. The twisting expressions on her face mirrored the agony of her fingers. She continued to speak.

"Butch hid pictures in the Bible. I found them that day."

"What day are you referring to?"

"The day after we went to watch the Tall Ships in Boston Harbor. The day after we had been happy."

Rachel's body began to rock forward and backward and her face crumpled into folds of pain.

Pearl rose to get Rachel a glass of water. She knew to let Rachel experience this struggle and not interrupt it. Suffering of this type needed to pass through a person's mind and body so it could exit and not return. The journey needed to be honored.

"What were the pictures like?" Pearl asked after Rachel had sipped some water and calmed her trembling.

"They were pictures of little girls, bad little girls."

Pearl didn't push for details. The guilt and shame that oppressed Rachel's soul bore down on her slumped body, almost visible in its crushing weight.

Though Willa had informed Pearl of the content of the Bible, Pearl had needed to hear it from Rachel. Enough for now.

"What did you do after you found the pictures?"

"I was tired so I went to bed."

"Did you sleep?"

"Yes." Rachel looked up at Pearl. "I hadn't slept for months but I fell asleep until Butch came home."

"What happened when Butch came home?"

Memory and fear etched their ragged trail in the lines of Rachel's face. "He was angry with me because supper wasn't ready."

"What did you do?"

"I rushed into the kitchen to cook. I got the cast iron skillet from the back room and set it on the stove. Then I realized I'd forgotten to thaw the chicken. Butch was furious."

"Then what happened?"

An invisible but absolutely solid wall of blankness dropped over Rachel's face and she stopped speaking.

Pearl knew the signs: terror taking charge once again, protecting the psyche from scenes too devastating to relive. She picked up the phone on her desk and called for the orderly. She studied Rachel's face, saw the vacant look in her eyes and made a note in the folder. It was true that sometimes a patient moved forward in rapid strides, but they also could move backwards just as speedily. She told herself that this retreat into emptiness for Rachel would likely be shorter than before. She would return. Time and patience were the keys.

CHAPTER 25

Cast in Iron

The breakfast dishes were washed and in the cupboard. Enoch had gone to work. Willa had the house to herself until supper time when she'd invited Jessie and Joe to join Enoch and her for a nice dinner. It was the only way she could think to help Jessie get through the last evening before her trial began.

Jessie had grown pale and lost weight in the past few weeks. Though Willa liked Joe and was pleased with the way he treated Jessie, she'd noticed tension between them, mostly a persistent irritation and morose attitude on Jessie's part.

When the pornographic pictures had been discovered in Butch's family Bible, Jessie's confidence in her acquittal had been restored. Her cheeks had regained some color and the mischievous sparkle had returned to her eyes.

But the facts were: Butch's pornographic pictures had no bearing on the murder trial, and without Rachel's testimony, not one shred of evidence could be found proving Butch had physically abused her.

Like common buzzards gathered on ragged branches of a dead tree, the damning realities had returned to roost and peck away at Jessie's certitude.

Thoughts of Jessie's upcoming trial and Rachel's institutionalization tormented Willa's every waking moment. In spite of those troubles, Willa began to find contentment in her routines around Rachel's home. Every room was spotless. The laundry was done, the ironing finished and supper planned. She slipped onto the bench of the organ that filled one end of the dining room. Once feeling vacant, at best half empty, the dining room had shrunk after the organ's arrival and one had to navigate carefully to avoid bruised shins.

She flipped through a notebook of pieces by Bach and settled on one of her favorites. She hummed a few phrases as she reviewed the pedals for "Jesu, Joy of Man's Desiring." Then she straightened her back and touched the keys of both registers with gentle affection.

She began playing, keeping the volume soft while her fingers ran through the rippling melody. As she switched to the broad chords, she increased the volume, letting the music sweep her away in its passion and beauty.

Later that afternoon, while Willa was humming a short piece by Paderewski (a favorite she used to make all her young piano students memorize) she went out on the front porch to collect the mail. She tripped over a pasteboard box sitting right under the black metal mailbox.

"Oh!" she cried as she slammed her hands against the wall and caught herself. Careless of the mailman to place the box so close to the door, she thought. She removed the mail from the mailbox and stooped to pick up the box, scanning the top for a return address.

When she set the box on the kitchen table she confirmed there was no *To* or *From* address. The box was closed but not sealed for shipping. Who would have dropped a box off here? she asked herself. She tucked the mail behind the toaster on the counter where Enoch would check through it and handle anything that pertained to Rachel.

She returned to the table and stared at the box again remembering it had been heavier than anticipated when she'd picked it up. *Guess I'll just look inside. lord knows there are no surprises left in my life.* She smiled at the irony of her assumptions. All my life, she thought as she pulled the flaps open, I've perceived my life as dull and prosaic. In light of these past few months, I would describe it as anything but.

When she looked down into the box, its contents didn't look so colorless either. There, filling the lower third of the brown box, lay her eclectic dish collection: shreds of lettuce leaves, cracked kernels of pale corn, and white-edged chunks of beet all jumbled together, shards of cheap pottery in a rainbow of colors like a psychedelic summary of her years with Floyd.

There had been times in her life, no, years of her life, when this wanton destruction of something she'd loved would have cut her to the core, when she would have burst forth in tears of hurt at the intended injury by the man she had loved.

Today, she simply stared down at the broken dishes, understood the cruel intent, thought briefly of the sadness that had motivated this sick behavior, and closed the box. She set the box out on the dryer in the back room and returned to the kitchen to prepare supper.

She shed not one tear as she scrubbed potatoes under the water then sat down at the kitchen table to peel them. The phone rang. It was Pearl. Willa listened intently as Pearl updated her on Rachel's situation and cautiously outlined a plan for transitioning Rachel to outpatient care over the next few months.

Willa returned to peeling the potatoes letting the long strips of brown skin drop into the pan in her lap. Visions of Rachel being home again raced through her head. "Hopefully late winter, early spring," Pearl had suggested, admonishing that everything hinged on Rachel's continued progress. Willa ran the caveats Pearl had listed through her jubilant mind over and over, painting over the therapist's concerns and warnings with scenes of herself at the dinner table surrounded by her three children, happy and free to be themselves, growing and learning and loving each other.

A slight damper fell over her spirit as her mother-in-law's nagging voice echoed in her memory. "Peel the potatoes very thinly, Willa. Remember, the vitamins are just under the skin."

Willa glanced up at the clock. Enoch would be home in thirty minutes. Hopefully Joe would be with him. Jessie had called and said she had been to the hairdresser and would be on time if she didn't get caught in traffic.

I won't start the chops until they all get here, she told herself. That way they'll be hot and juicy. She put the pot of potatoes on the stove to boil and began cutting up fresh vegetables for salad.

The pungent smell of lemon and cloves was still escaping from the mincemeat pie she'd baked earlier in the afternoon as she set four places at the gray Formica table. For a moment she bent closer to the dulled boomerang pattern and remembered how she and Floyd had been so excited when the new chrome and Formica dinette set had been delivered back in Cleveland, Ohio in 1956. "You've got quite a bit of mileage on you," she told the old table, patting the smooth surface and smiling.

She heard the sound of crunching gravel in the driveway and stood on tiptoe to look out the window over the sink. Looks like Joe followed Enoch from the station, she mused. I hope Jessie isn't late.

"Grab that large cast iron skillet on the wall by the washer," Willa called to Enoch as he came through the back door.

"Greetings to you, too," Enoch said pleasantly as he laid his officer's cap on a high shelf and reached for the skillet.

"Hi, Joe," Willa called. "Glad you two didn't get held up at work."

"This one?" Enoch asked entering the kitchen holding the heavy skillet vertically as it had hung on the wall. Willa came toward him reaching out to take the skillet. "It's too heavy for you to handle. Where do you want me to put it?"

Something on the edge of the skillet caught Enoch's eye. He raised the skillet higher and drew it closer to study it carefully. "Yuck. There's crap on the edge." Enoch held the pan toward the ceiling light to scrutinize the dried residue. Joe edged around

Enoch and peered up at the suspended frying pan. "I thought Rachel kept everything immaculate," Enoch said.

"Give it to me," Willa said, reaching for the pan again. "I'll scrub it up. You two go wash up; supper will be ready in a jiff."

"Don't touch that pan," Joe said, flinging his arms outward to block Willa. He and Enoch exchanged glances and stood there for a tense moment, both staring at the suspended skillet under the fluorescent light.

Slightly miffed at the intrusion on her plans for a nice dinner, Willa said, "If I don't get cooking, the potatoes will be done too early. They'll turn to mush."

"Don't touch that skillet, Mother," Enoch said in a firm voice. He set the skillet down on the table and stood back, allowing Joe to take a closer look while he held out his arms to keep Willa away.

"What's the matter with you two?" Willa demanded. "I can wash it."

Joe stood back and stared at the skillet like Moses descended from the mountain to find the Hebrews worshiping a golden calf. "That's it!" he said in a low voice of amazement. "That explains why there was no blood on the copper pan." He glanced at Enoch and back at the skillet. "She killed Butch with this iron skillet. This is the murder weapon!"

"What murder weapon?" Jessie asked as she entered the kitchen and heard Joe's last remark. She tossed her jacket and scarf on a kitchen chair.

As Joe turned to Jessie, the childish embroidery on the wall caught his eye. "That's it!" he cried louder, pointing to the framed sampler. "'*A Place For Everything and Everything in its Place*'. That's what happened! She put the skillet back."

Joe seized Jessie in a frantic bear hug, gripping her with such enthusiasm she cried out, "Let me go! What in hell's the matter with you?" She pushed Joe back good-naturedly then sensed the tension in the room. She glanced first at Enoch standing guard over an iron skillet on the table, then at Willa, slumped helplessly in a chair at the far end of the table, her eyes riveted to the black frying pan.

"Nobody move. I'll be right back," Joe said and dashed out the back door.

Jessie started to walk toward the table but was stopped dead in her tracks by the look in Enoch's eyes. "What the hell's wrong with you?" she asked.

"I think you know," Enoch said softening his accusatory stare into one of puzzlement and wonder. "Why'd you do it?"

"Do what?" Jessie eased around him and pulled out a chair to sit down at the far end of the table. "What's going on here, Mother?"

"I think Enoch believes you lied about the murder weapon."

"Not quite," Enoch said cryptically as Joe returned to the kitchen.

While the pot of potatoes boiled dry on the stove, Joe used a bright flashlight and magnifying glass from his crime kit to study the residue stuck to the edge of the iron skillet. "Hair," he mumbled. "Definitely hair." The room was silent though Jessie's eyes were screaming questions at Willa and Enoch who couldn't take their eyes off Joe.

Without looking up from his examination of the skillet, Joe began talking in a low voice. "Like I told you weeks ago, Jessie, I think you should write a human-interest story, you know, the one where the reporter takes the blame for the death of her brother-in-law but the detective doesn't believe her?"

"Oh!" Willa cried, jumping to her feet and rushing to the stove.

"What, Mother?" Enoch cried, jolted out of his trance watching Joe.

"Can't you smell it? I've burned the potatoes!" Willa grabbed two thick potholders and rushed the smoking pan to the sink, dumping the charred potatoes into a colander and turning on cold water to cool the pot.

Enoch went over and opened the window over the sink to release the acrid odor into the cold November air.

"I don't understand," Willa said, turning away from the sink and leaning back against the counter. "Why would you hang up a dirty skillet after you killed someone with it?" She looked at Jessie like a reasonable answer was forthcoming.

"She didn't, Mother." Enoch said. "Rachel did."

"Rachel hung it up? Dirty? Why would she do that? To protect Jessie? I don't understand at all." This was simply too much. Willa wilted.

"Mother," Enoch said kindly and slowly. "Rachel killed Butch, not Jessie."

The miracle Willa had been praying for! The truth! Willa raised her head and spoke rapidly, "We don't have to turn in the skillet. Now that we know Jessie didn't do it; she will be acquitted. Rachel's sick now but when she's better, she can come home and everything will be all right." She searched the others' faces for agreement.

"We can't do that," Enoch said, looking at Joe for confirmation. "It's evidence."

Suddenly Willa jumped up and ran around the table. She threw her arms around her younger daughter. "I'm so glad you didn't do it, but what are we going to do?" Frantically, she looked at Joe. "If we turn in the skillet, Rachel gets blamed. If we don't, Jessie will go to prison. I can't make a choice between two daughters!" She looked up at Enoch slowly edging closer to the skillet and cried, "How can you choose between two sisters?"

"I don't think we'll need to do that," Joe said, pulling out a chair next to Jessie and sitting down.

As though reaching for life preservers on a storm-tossed sea, Willa and Enoch took seats, peppering Joe with questions as they settled around the table, leaving a wide gap of space between themselves and the offensive skillet.

Joe took Jessie's hand, cradled it in his own, and began to speak. "Until the crime lab confirms this is the murder weapon, I can only make assumptions." He looked directly at Jessie who had begun to weep though she held her head high and fought to blink back the flood of tears.

Willa grabbed some paper napkins from the holder in the middle of the table and handed them to Jessie.

"I didn't know what else to do," Jessie said, looking around the table. "I've made a terrible mess."

Jessie laid her head down on her folded arms and sobbed.

Joe slid closer to Jessie and put his arm around her heaving shoulders. Speaking calmly he addressed Jessie and her family. "I'm not schooled in the law, as you all know, but I believe this will be put to rest." He glanced at Jessie's bowed head and patted her sleek black hair. She sat upright and wiped her face with the crinkly napkins. "Jessie will likely come under fire for making false statements and misleading a criminal investigation. Those things can be dealt with."

"But poor Rachel," Willa cried. "At supper I was going to tell you all that Pearl called this afternoon and said that Rachel had had a setback this week but she believed a loving home setting would help her more than staying in an institution. She's hoping to transition Rachel to outpatient care, perhaps early next year. Now what will happen to Rachel?"

"I can't tell you for sure," Joe said. "With the evidence we have uncovered since Butch's death, I don't think the state will be in a rush to press charges." He looked at Jessie and smiled. "I believe you were right about Butch and I believe that with time, Rachel will be able to tell us what you knew in your gut." He gave her a little squeeze. "You always get the story."

For the first time since she'd entered the kitchen, Jessie smiled.

Joe hugged Jessie closer and said, "About that human-interest story I suggested you write?" He gave her a crooked smile. "You might want to rewrite the phrase 'taking a liking to the reporter.'

You could say the detective is 'falling in love with the reporter.'"
Joe bent down and gave Jessie a kiss on her wet cheek.

Enoch put his arm around Willa and hugged her.

The End

ABOUT
JEANINE COLLINS MALARSKY

Jeanine Collins Malarsky was born on the shores of Cayuga Lake in upstate New York in 1944. The middle daughter of a peripatetic dairy farmer, she was moved from house to house and state to state east of the Mississippi. She left home to attend college in New England where she met her husband and found a permanent home near Boston, Massachusetts.

Ms. Malarsky spent thirty-six years in business management, focusing on financial accounting and computer systems, including twenty-two years owning and operating her own company. Following years devoted to gourmet cooking, sewing, and raising two children, she is now retired and living with her husband, a retired airline pilot.

She has traveled extensively including most of Europe and the Far East, indulging in her love of history and learning. An avid lifelong student of human behavior, she now devotes her energies to travel, reading and writing.